Tales of Love and Courage
from Milkweed Manor

I0646523

The Guardians

Tales of Love and Courage From Milkweed Manor

by Kaaren Poole

Front cover and all illustrations by Kaaren Poole

Book design by Kaaren Poole

ISBN: 978-1-7340331-2-0

First printing edition 2019

Kaaren Poole
5280 Old French Town Road
Shingle Springs, CA 95682

www.kaarenpoole.com

Preface

I'm a hopeless animal enthusiast. I gravitate towards the lone dog working the crowded room, the cat napping in the corner of the bookstore, the glorious rose garden's resident duck. Animals never fail to bring a smile to my face and joy to my heart—the perfect antidote for a bad day or boost for a good one. If you share any of these feelings, I predict you'll enjoy reading this book as much as I enjoyed pouring my heart into writing and illustrating it.

The first seeds of "Milkweed Manor" sprouted as I found myself imagining stories about the ceramic animal figurines I was sculpting for my Etsy shop, TheFoxesGarden. First it was the squirrel girls, Effie and Lily, on their Great Mushroom Hunt. Then it was Aunt Audrey the badger, collecting marvelous crystals as she dug her burrows. Then a poor beggar rat who in time morphed into Colwyn, the main character of this collection of stories.

When I began, writing was a disjoint effort with no particular goal. I wrote the stories as they came to life for me, led by a cast of characters that kept expanding as I imagined a community of animals living in the forest behind Milkweed Manor, an old English manor house. When I had eight stories, it was time to arrange them in a rational sequence. Although there were many characters overall, each story had a limited cast. I ordered the stories in the same sequence in which the characters stepped on stage. Now I had a first draft.

Then "Milkweed Manor" fell by the wayside. There were so many creative projects calling to me—paintings, collages, needle felted animals, ceramic figures—there just didn't seem to be room for a long-term project like a book.

The book remained in my mind though, and one morning someone asked me what the book was about. I hadn't really thought about that, but the answer came to me as soon as the question was asked. Fundamentally, this collection of stories is what I call "gentle animal advocacy." The stories show how animal lives are affected by living in the shadow of man. I realized "Milkweed Manor" would give me an opportunity to give animals a voice.

Often, especially in children's books, animals are characters in a story to teach a lesson to humans about their own lives. "All the animals get along so well. They help each other, listen to each other, and work towards common goals. Well, people should do that too!" But I have an additional goal with this book. The stories and characters may invite you to think more deeply about how we treat animals. Consequences of direct actions—such as the way we care for our pets—are obvious.

But there are also unintended and/or unseen consequences such as displacement due to human development, or hunger due to removal of a food source. Thinking about these consequences gives us the opportunity to seek better ways—changes in human behaviors and attitudes that work to animals' benefit. That's my message and hope behind these stories. And if animals could speak in a soft voice, I think that's what they'd say too.

With a clear understanding of my purpose, in the autumn of 2018 I embraced the project of writing and illustrating "Tales of Love and Courage from Milkweed Manor" as one so important to me that I was willing to put my other creative efforts aside, focus on this one, and see it through. I'm glad I did. It's been a wonderful adventure, and here it is for you to enjoy.

It's funny how when one finally finishes something that's been such a long, near-to-the-heart journey, a flood of mixed emotions hits. But why mixed? Shouldn't it all be good? A feeling of accomplishment! A pride in staying the course and finishing! A mother's love for that creature I brought into being! Anticipation of sales and praise! Well, yes, all of those. But also, a deep sadness. It's over... Worry. What if no one likes it? That lost-in-space feeling. What do I do now?

What do I do now? Volume 2, "Dark Days at Milkweed Manor," coming in 2020.

About the Illustrations

I didn't begin the illustrations until I had written the entire book and finished many editing passes. I wanted the text to be finished enough that I could select which passages I would illustrate with confidence those passages would remain unchanged. That process took several months, but during that period I split my time between working on the text and drawing. I worked in a sketchbook, drawing the animals that would be my characters, depicting each one over and over again in a variety of poses, studying proportions and characteristics. It was a worthwhile, as well as rewarding effort because by the time I started the actual illustrations, I felt I knew the animals well. Of course, there was still the occasional question to answer. "Once again, how are those rat whiskers arranged?" But it wasn't so often to disrupt to flow of creating the illustrations.

Which medium to use was a difficult decision. Graphite is my favorite and I thought long and hard about using pencil drawings—the simplicity appealed to me. In the end, I couldn't turn my back on color! But I knew I didn't want the look of paintings. I still wanted the look of drawing, so I developed a process that gave me the look of tinted drawings. To me, it has an old-fashioned look which is in keeping with the "voice" of the stories.

I worked each illustration in two phases—drawing, then adding color. For the drawing, I used HB pencil on Stonehenge drawing paper, then added 2B pencil for the darks. Before I could add the color, I had to prepare the drawings to receive it. This involved 'fixing' the graphite with spray workable fixative, then adhering the drawing paper to Crescent Perfect Mount board. This made the drawing stiff enough to accept paint. For the color, I used thin washes of transparent acrylic paint. Through my previous work with mixed media, I've learned acrylic washes work nicely over acrylic medium, so as the final preparation for color, I coated the drawing with two coats of acrylic matte medium to seal the paper. Then I could add washes of color.

What great fun this whole adventure has been. Thanks for joining me!

Kaaren Poole

DRAMATIS

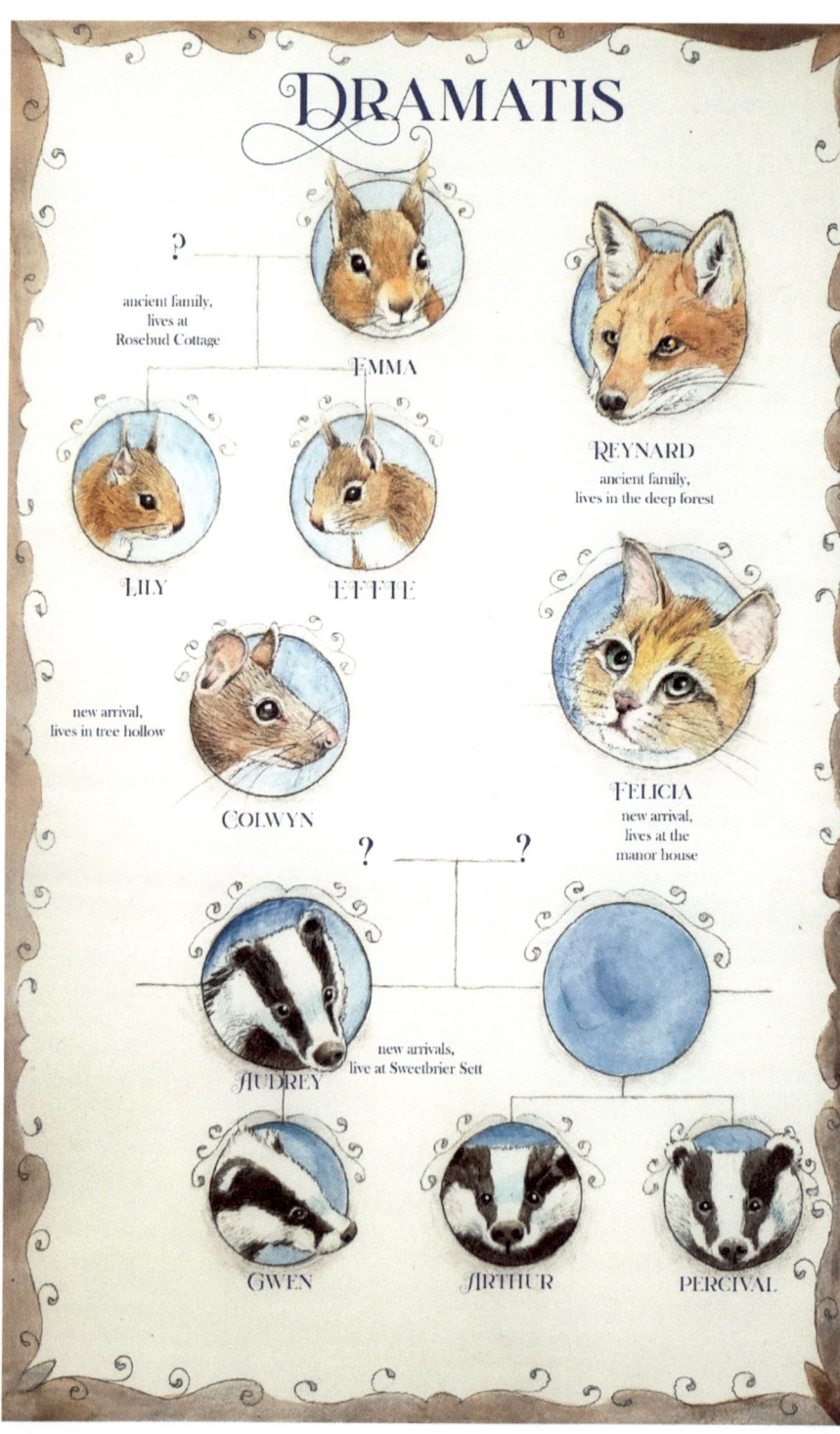

?
ancient family,
lives at
Rosebud Cottage

EMMA

REYNARD
ancient family,
lives in the deep forest

LILY

EFFIE

new arrival,
lives in tree hollow

COLWYN

FELICIA
new arrival,
lives at the
manor house

?   **?**

new arrivals,
live at Sweetbrier Sett

AUDREY

GWEN

ARTHUR

PERCIVAL

Personae

THOMAS

MEG

old family,
lives in a hedge

SOPHIE

CARMEN

THEA

new arrival,
lives, initially, with the squirrels

familial relationship, if any, between
Rupert and Rose unknown

RUPERT

ancient
inhabitants,
live in the
Norman tower

ROSE

ROXANNE

new arrival,
lives at the Mercantile

GLENNA

GRAHAM

ancient family,
lives in the
Inn at Ivy Knoll

VICIOUS

ancient family,
lives in the deep forest
with Reynard

EVIE

Dedicated to Michele, Audrey,
Sophie, Carmen, and Omar

IN LOVING MEMORY OF
MEGAN.
I LOVE YOU
ALWAYS AND FOREVER

The Stories

Every bird must leave the nest.
Circumstances differ, but the results are the
same: embarking on this marvelous journey we
call life.

In which Colwyn Arrives at Milkweed Manor

It was one of those perfect soft spring nights in Hawthorne village. Fireflies danced in the honeysuckle which, in full bloom, released its heavenly fragrance into the balmy air. An owl hooted in the distance. Spangled with stars and set with a quarter moon, the sky shifted from lavender to periwinkle and finally to the deepest purple. It seemed so peaceful.

A villager strolling along Main Street that night might have noticed Mama standing in the window of the tiny burrow beneath the apothecary steps. She held little Lucy in her arms. Mama didn't seem to notice that the baby was wriggling restlessly.

Her anxious gaze was fixed on the street, her glittering eyes reflecting the light of the streetlamp. She twitched her whiskers in a vain attempt to stem the tears stinging her eyes. *Where could Papa be?* she kept asking herself. *He's never been this late. He should have been back long ago with our supper!* She was desperately worried, and rapidly becoming afraid.

Lucy started squeaking, and Mama, with no small effort, gathered herself.

She dried her eyes and turned away from the window. Tucking Lucy tenderly into her highchair, she managed a weak smile for the rest of the children sitting around the table. The candles which had been winking cheerfully earlier in the evening had now burned down so low they were nearly out. The room was dim and gloomy. As Mama scanned from little face to little face, she saw in each hunger, exhaustion, and distress in varying degree—a spectrum of emotions that nearly broke her heart.

Colwyn, the oldest, slumped in his chair on the far side of the table. The entire time Mama had stood vigil at the window, his attention had been focused on her, watching for a sign she saw Papa approaching. But no such sign had come. He recognized her efforts to calm her face and voice, and he did the same.

"Mama, the little ones are so hungry. I know it'd be better to wait for Papa, but could we just finish up the crusts he brought us last night? I think he'd forgive us for starting without him."

"Of course. You're right. Why don't you help me fetch them?" She gazed at her beloved family and spoke softly. "We all should get something in our tummies, then get some sleep. Our worrying isn't bringing Papa home! There's no doubt been some unforeseen delay, and all will be better in the morning."

* * * * *

But things were not better in the morning. Papa was still missing. Everyone got through the day as best they could, moment by moment, step by step. Then the next day, and the ones after that. The younger the child, the more quickly he or she began to recover. Within a month, the younger children were functioning more or less normally. Mama and Colwyn, however, were still suffering.

Mama had fourteen mouths to feed. Though all the children helped as best they could, times were tough and oh, so sad. It was an unending struggle to put food on the table and clothes on the young rats' backs. She was stretched too thin.

Meanwhile, it didn't take long for Colwyn to figure out why Papa hadn't returned that night. It was because of him! Not too long ago, he had begun to feel unfamiliar stirrings inside, questions and confusions he hadn't felt when he was younger. He came to resent the rules and was rebellious. Most of the time he was sullen and quiet. When he did speak, it was to argue with his parents. *Papa clearly couldn't take it anymore. He left to get away from me.* That was how Colwyn came to understand his father's disappearance. With this revelation, his behaviour got even worse. *Since I've been so severely punished for being bad, I may as well be really bad!* It was a child's twisted logic.

Colwyn didn't confine his bad behaviour to home life. He took it to school as well. He pulled the girls' tails and stole treats from their lunches. He tripped the smaller boys, then made fun of them when they cried. He bullied everyone on the playground, and soon most of the children dreaded recess. He was loud and rowdy in the library. He was rude to his teachers. He was in trouble all the time.

Then one morning, just for fun, he pushed a classmate. The poor little creature fell face first. Struggling to her feet, she confronted Colwyn with two sad black eyes, an angry swollen lump on her forehead, and her pink hair bow dirty and askew. She was crying piteously—tears of pain but, more than that, indignation.

He pulled the girls' tails

Colwyn knew he would be in big trouble this time. It was so unfair! He was just having a little fun. How was he to know she was so clumsy? And, to make matters worse, the 'injured' party was Emily, his sisters' best friend. He would no doubt be severely taken to task, so he started planning his defense. *I pushed her from behind and didn't realise it was Emily!* No, that didn't sound right...

* * * * *

Sure enough, that evening Emily's mum came to the house to complain about Colwyn's brutality. *Brutality?* Colwyn was indignant. *I was just playing a little prank!* Then she announced that, in future, her daughter could have no contact with Colwyn or his siblings. Mama was mortified.

Colwyn's sisters began to squeak and wail! "No! We love Emily! She's our best friend! We can't live without her!" And with that, they ran from the room and flung themselves hopelessly on their beds. Colwyn bit his lip and suddenly found the pattern on the carpet very interesting. Despite the excuses he made to himself, he knew he had gone too far.

* * * * *

None of the rats slept well that night. Colwyn's sisters, still stinging from Emily's mum's pronouncement, sobbed and snuffled miserably. His brothers, whose sleep was continually interrupted by the snuffles and sobs, were getting really annoyed. Mama stared into the darkness, missing Papa and feeling so alone in her troubles.

As for Colwyn, he lay awake gazing out the window at the far-away stars. They looked so pretty and peaceful. Through smothered sobs, he muttered, "Peaceful." Precisely the opposite of how he felt. Not only had his atrocious behaviour caused Papa to leave, but now he had shamed Mama and separated his sisters from their best friend. He felt terrible.

He looked at the moon, and his mind began to wander. *The moon's light falls everywhere, so it must be falling on happier places than this. I wonder where those places are? I wonder what's happening there and who lives there.* His young mind began to explore that idea. *I wonder if there could be a life for me in one of those happier places? I've hurt everyone here. Maybe it would be better somewhere else. I could have a new start and no one there would know what a bad rat I've been, and I could be a good rat again...* With that, he drifted into a fitful sleep. He dreamt about being in a beautiful place, sunny and warm, with other animals who were his friends. Life was so good there...

* * * * *

The next morning, Colwyn awoke with the conviction that he needed a new direction.

As Mama was laying out breakfast, Colwyn walked up behind her and laid his paw on her shoulder. He was so nervous about what he was about to say that his legs were trembling. "Mama, I need to talk to you." She turned and gave him her full attention, but his eyes were wide with apprehension. His voice was shaky and higher pitched than usual. "You've always stood by me. A rat couldn't have a better mama, and I love you so much!" He looked down, wrung his paws, and shifted from one foot to the other. "But everything has been so hard lately. I know my bad behaviour is a weight on your heart and I feel terrible about it. You have enough problems with Papa gone without me constantly disrupting everything." His voice was close to breaking. "I've decided it would be best for everyone if I left."

Tears shone in Mama's eyes, and she covered her face with her paws. She was not expecting this! *Everything Colwyn said is true. Everything except that it would best for everyone if he left. It certainly would not be best for me. I can't image another loss. What can I say to change his mind?*

Try as she might to remain calm, her wavering voice betrayed her emotions. She gently took Colwyn's front paws in hers. "My dear, yes, your behaviour has been difficult lately, but this reaction to losing Papa is natural. In time, you'll feel better, things will be smoother for you, and you'll rediscover your previous charming self. And in the meantime, there is no way my life would be better without you!" In a quiet voice she doubted Colwyn could hear, she added "I don't want you to leave!"

But he was determined. "I know I'll miss you and my brothers and sisters terribly. But I really must get a new start. Without a major change, I'll simply stay on a path that can only end in disaster. I must go. And since my mind is made up, delay will only make leaving more painful."

* * * * *

A mere hour later, and after the shedding of many tears, the young rat slung a pack holding his few worldly belongings over his shoulder and set off. He longed to turn around for one more glimpse of his family but doubted he would have the strength to continue if he did. *One paw in front of the other. Just concentrate on that! That's the ticket...* With grim determination, he travelled the village street, then headed into the countryside.

He didn't have a destination in mind and didn't even know which direction to go. But the hopeful light of the rising sun beckoned to him. His mood brightened and, determining to leave his cares behind, he purposely strode east.

It was only a short time before he left the village behind, and it wasn't long till he came to a small stream. The slowly moving water burbled cheerfully, winding effortlessly among cat tails and around shiny wet rocks. Light sparked off the water, and the sun warmed his face. He stood still for a bit, twitched his whiskers, and sighed deeply, appreciating the first moment of happiness he'd felt in a long time. Since the stream seemed to know where it was going, he decided to go there too.

He followed as it wound through open meadows and small copses. He saw and heard and smelled so many wonders! Yes, of course he knew about birds, but here by the stream he saw many kinds that he'd never seen in the village. And their songs! Some sweet, some insistent, some raucous. He felt he understood them—cheer, caution, playfulness. Colorful butterflies and iridescent dragonflies fluttered and hovered over the water. Patches of sweet-smelling pink and white flowers studded the stream banks. Bees hummed in busy contentment. Squirrels jumped through the branches above him, dislodging showers of leaves. Unseen creatures rustled in the undergrowth.

Now the stream widened. The water flowed slowly and quietly, lapping gently at its banks. Soon after, it rushed faster, and as it squeezed between narrowing banks its voice became louder and stronger. Occasionally there was a flash of light as the sun glinted off a silvery fish.

Colwyn was so enchanted with his travels that the morning passed quickly. The sun was high before he noticed he was tired and hungry. *Bullying the children at school,* he chuckled to himself, *was a lot less exhausting than walking all morning!* But then he caught himself. *It's not funny, Colwyn! Remember you've vowed to leave your bad behavior behind, so don't romanticise it. Straighten up!*

Ahead, just as the stream entered a stand of oak trees, a large blackberry bush arched its branches over the water, forming a shady shelter on the grassy bank. *A perfect spot for a snack and a little rest, then back to my journey!* Colwyn stretched out in the shade and enjoyed some berries. *Yum, they're so juicy and sweet— scrumptious!* Everything was quiet except for the warbling of the stream and the buzzing of the bees. Suddenly, in the quiet, he felt sad. He couldn't help but think about being with his brothers and sisters and how every bedtime and naptime they would lie down together in a cozy soothing pile of fur. How lonely it was without them!

He fell asleep under the berry bushes.

A small group of sparrows alighted on the berry branches. They chirped excitedly as they feasted on the ripe, fragrant fruit. *They sound truly happy. I wonder if I'll be happy someday...*

The birds were lively and cheerful, but Colwyn was still sad. Soon, though, the warm afternoon sun had him nodding off.

The young traveller slept soundly in his hideaway, his paws or whiskers twitching now and then as he dreamed. The intended nap was becoming a night's sleep. The sun sank as day surrendered to twilight. Foxes emerged from their dens. Mice scurried through last winter's fallen leaves, and skunks trolled the stream bank. Above, owls watched from their perches in the ancient oaks and beeches. The sky darkened to indigo, and wispy clouds slid silently across the moon. Tree branches swayed with a light wind, their shadows faintly patterning the ground. After an initial burst of activity, the creatures settled into the night's routine until several hours later a coral pink glow spread upwards from the eastern horizon. The songbirds awoke, their sweet voices greeting the day. Golden light brushed the crests of the hills and lit the tips of the trees. It was the signal for the night creatures to withdraw to their safe sleeping places, leaving the forest to the creatures of the day.

* * * * *

Colwyn awoke to a bright new morning. His first thoughts were of his mother and brothers and sisters. He missed them so much! Tears stung his eyes. For a few sad moments, his courage failed, and he wanted to go back home. But as the sunlight stretched across the grass and filtered through the branches of the berry bush where he lay, clarity returned. He had made his decision wisely. Hardship and doubt were inevitable, but he knew he could overcome them. After all, he was strong, just like Papa had been! *How I miss him!* He ate a few berries, put a few more in his pack, and off he went, continuing down the bank of the stream, ready for what the day would bring.

Around mid-morning, he saw something new—small docks, some with small boats tied up to them. The stream grew steadily wider until it was so wide that, although he was a good swimmer, he doubted he could swim all the way across. As he walked on, he noticed larger boats tied to larger docks. *Interesting. Makes me wonder what's ahead.*

With that thought something bright caught his eye. It was a vivid white and deep blue striped object. Naturally cautious, he slowed his pace. *What is it? An animal? Is it dangerous?* He would need to get quite a bit closer to see it clearly. He moved carefully and quietly, hoping he would see this creature before the creature saw him! Finally, he recognized the colourful object as an elderly, rather crusty looking rat wearing a nautical striped shirt. He recognized the style from several photos in the family album. His ancestors had been sea rats.

After a bit more than twenty-four hours on his own, Colwyn was already so hungry for companionship that he overcame his natural avoidance of strange rats and approached. "Hello there, sir! What a lovely day for enjoying this fine view!"

The old rat, used to a lifetime of crowded conditions on board ship, was habitually appreciative of some company, and invited Colwyn to sit a spell and enjoy a chat. "Welcome, young man. Old Morris here! I'm a ship rat—retired long ago, but still drawn to the docks." And with a nod of his grey head, added, "S'pose I always will be!"

Colwyn sat down beside Old Morris who, delighted to have an audience, began to spin colourful stories of life at sea, including uncomfortably detailed descriptions of more than one brush with death! It seemed Old Morris had an endless supply of adventures to relate. But after several harrowing tales of shipwrecks and other dangers at sea, all of which brought a twinkle to the old rat's eye, the old salt visibly tired.

He paused, smiled, and fixed his knowing eyes on Colwyn. "You know, lad, if you continue along this river you'll come to a town at the edge of big water. Just use the name 'Old Morris' and you'll find many opportunities for a life at sea—perfect for a young adventurer like yourself!"

Since Colwyn felt queasy just looking at the boats bobbing up and down alongside the dock, it was clear a life at sea was not for him! "Thank you, sir. It's tempting indeed! But I'm looking for a peaceful forest to settle in, a forest where there are other animals and life is good."

"Too bad! But that being the case, you should alter your course and go that way!" He shakily pointed away from the river, but thankfully on the same side of the water where they sat. "That's where the richest forests are."

Colwyn pulled a few berries from his pack and gave them to Old Morris, who was delighted with the gift. "Helps with scurvy," he muttered, leaving Colwyn to wonder what that was, but, now anxious to be on his way, he chose not to inquire. Instead, he bid farewell, hoisted his pack onto his back, and set out in the direction the sea rat pointed.

* * * * *

That was a pleasant interlude, and useful too. I learned I don't want to be a sea rat! He smiled to himself. As he walked the morning away, he noticed the landscape was changing. The light grew clearer and the colors brighter. Delicate flowers he had never seen before graced the meadows. *The trees are so large here!* They might have seemed intimidating, but instead were majestic, casting intricate shadows that made the ground sparkle with light and dark patches. A delicate scent perfumed the air, one that Colwyn couldn't identify. He was approaching a lake—a lake of the clearest sky blue with a surface so mirror-smooth that it reflected the myriad hovering dragonflies like shimmering jewels.

Soft music—a harp, he thought—greeted him as he approached the water's edge. Colwyn stood transfixed, peering into the water and wondering what this magical place could be. Just then, an amazingly beautiful head and flawless shoulders rose above the water's surface. Colwyn was startled, but quickly calmed in the presence of this perfect creature. In the bright light of early afternoon, her chestnut fur shone as though dusted with tiny diamonds. Her deep chocolate eyes flashed with an inner light. Her small delicate ears mimicked the most beautiful seashells. A filet of freshwater pearls encircled her perfect forehead and clusters of water hyacinth settled like a cloud of lavender and periwinkle over her head. Colwyn was awestruck.

"Greetings, young sir. I am pleased you stopped here on your travels. You are perhaps wondering what this place is and who I am. Let me satisfy your curiosity.

"You've entered an enchanted forest, thick with the most precious trees of our land and peopled with extraordinary creatures: pale deer, black swans, white boar, and many other sorts. This crystalline lake on whose banks you stand is its center, its living breathing heart. At its deepest point, a hidden spring feeds it and is the source of all its power. I am Belisama, the lake's guardian spirit. I've watched over this lake from the very beginning of time and have ancient mystical powers, among them, a keen perception. My perception reveals to me that you are on a most significant journey. You left your family and the home of your birth—a difficult and painful decision—and set out to find a better life. Quite a remarkable and courageous undertaking. But it's more. I tell you that you've set out to find your destiny, and so you will! Keep your heart true, and your future will be great. You will accomplish many remarkable things and bring both comfort and enjoyment to many."

Belisama danced and wove through the waters, playful and yet graceful as only otters can be. She finished her delightful dance by gliding up the lake bank to where Colwyn stood. The beauty's glorious eyes met his, and he knew she could see into his very soul. Ordinarily he would have been too shy to speak, but nothing was ordinary in the presence of this fantastical creature. He was surprisingly at ease.

"My life at home became so difficult I decided to leave. Now I realize I left without knowing where I was going. Though I'm enjoying my wanderings, what I really want is to find a place to settle and build a new life. But I'm afraid I won't know when or where to end my journey." Colwyn's cheeks burned rosy and bright as the Lady took his paws in hers and blessed him with a gentle kiss on his forehead.

"Your heart will tell you when you've reached the place you're destined to be." With that, she wished him safe travels and, as she disappeared under the surface of the magical lake, bid her golden dragonflies escort him to the edge of the enchanted wood.

eternal mystical being,
lives in the lake in the enchanted forest

ßELISAM ƒ

* * * * *

As he continued on his way, forest gave way to meadow, then meadow to forest. There were hollows and copses, thickets and ponds and stream banks. Many of those places could be pleasant to settle in, yet none seemed quite right. After a long day of travel, fatigue, both of body and mind, began taking its toll. He needed a rest, and soon spotted a low grassy bank shaded by sheltering trees, an inviting setting for a nap. There was brush towards the top of the bank which would hide him from view. Gathering fallen leaves into a soft pile, he lay down and promptly fell into a sound sleep.

Just beyond the bank where Colwyn lay napping was a charming clearing in a small hollow. Hazelnut trees, highly regarded by the animals in the area, ringed the hollow. Not only were the nuts delicious, but the trees had a comforting spirituality about them. Legend held that the sacred origin of the world was a pool at the feet of a similar grove. The local forest community held its most important celebrations in this clearing.

Late that afternoon, as Colwyn continued to sleep, the undergrowth rustled and quivered as a pair of young badgers burst excitedly into the far side of the clearing. Soon, more animals, all of them excited but much calmer than the badger boys, joined them. There were squirrels, a pair of crows, and a family of mice. Some were carrying bundles. A pretty young hare, accompanied by her elderly parents, proudly carried a beautifully decorated cake on a rustic platter of woven willow branches.

The sound of voices woke Colwyn. He crawled further into the underbrush to hide. Though naturally cautious he was also curious, so after a moment, he peered through the branches. He was surprised to see the gathering of forest animals. After watching for a while, it seemed safe enough, so he rose to a more comfortable sitting position to better observe what was happening. Just then the last animals arrived—first, an unfamiliar creature with a masked face and ringed tail, then two badgers, one young and the other older. The badger girl, led by the adult, wore a pink dotted Swiss party-dress and a crown of flowers. She flashed a wide smile at the other animals. This girl was clearly the guest of honor at whatever this gathering might be.

At the guest of honor's arrival, the squirrel family unwrapped the bundles, spread a cloth over a low flat rock, and set out a buffet of tempting treats. Into the center of the display, the young hare proudly placed her decorated cake. All the animals cheered, apparently the signal for the mouse family chorus to approach the badger. They arranged themselves in a semi-circle around her. The oldest child, the leader, stood in front of the others. She glanced right, then left at the assembled singers. Assured that she had each child's attention, she uttered a soft, precisely pitched squeak. She marked time with three waves of her paw, then the choir burst into song. "Squeak squeak squeak squeak squeak squ-e-a-k...squeak, squeak Gwen, ..." Colwyn thought it might be a piercing rendition of "Happy Birthday!" *Very sweet! And the badger girl's name must be 'Gwen.'*

12

The girl was clearly the guest of honor.

The birthday girl served the cake. The animals helped themselves to the other treats and sat together enjoying the food, laughing and talking, and telling stores. *What a wonderful community!* Colwyn mused. *They're having so much fun and they all get along so well!* This harmonious atmosphere was quite different from what he had been used to lately. He reflected, though, that the boasting, rude behavior, and bullying which had caused so much trouble were in fact, his own! *This is one of those happier places I dreamed about when I was back home.* Then Belisama's prophetic words came back to him. 'Your heart will tell you when you've reached the place you're destined to be.'

Colwyn stepped quietly into the clearing. All the animals turned to him.

"Hello, everyone! I'm a traveller, looking for a new home and a better life. I've been watching your celebration, and I'm inspired by all of you." The animals circled him, greeting him warmly. He paused for a moment before shyly adding, "Perhaps you'll let me stay with you in this forest."

The animals answered in a single voice. "We saw you sleeping there, and then we saw you watching. You seemed lost—perhaps a weary traveller. As for staying, we thought you'd never ask! You're welcome here!"

The mice, thinking Colwyn was a very large and strong mouse, squeaked excitedly. "Come with us! We have just the place for you!"

The mouse family lived in a cozy nest of leaves and twigs in the branches of a hedge near a large oak tree. There was a hollow a few feet up the tree trunk, and that was where they settled Colwyn. The hollow was lined with soft fragrant grasses. He curled up in them, comfortable, warm, and more peaceful than he'd felt in a long time. Lying there, he could see the moon through the opening of the hollow.

I'm so grateful I found this place and the animals have welcomed me. And it's so important to leave my bad behavior behind. I must remind myself every morning this is a new beginning and a new me. The old me, actually—the sweet, caring rat I was before loss changed me.

The sadness struck again. *I miss my family so much! Moon, you shine on them tonight just as you shine on me. Are they alright?* A tear rolled down his cheek. *Do they miss me? I hope they do, but not so much it hurts...*

* * * * *

Late that night, the animal community's two guardian crows, Rupert and Rose, perched on the edge of Colwyn's hollow and, as he slept, delivered a message. "Colwyn," Rose whispered, "we've just come from your mother. We took her your love. We told her you are well and have found a new home. She and your brothers and sisters are well, love you, miss you, and wish you happiness. Your father watches over you from the world of the spirits. You are loved, Colwyn." And so, his heart at rest, Colwyn settled in the community in the forest behind Milkweed Manor.

What is family? At best, the ultimate support
group where love is unconditional, and each
member is always there for every other. But, for
whatever reason, the family into which one is
born doesn't always fill that bill. In the end,
family is where you find it

In Which Colwyn's Hollow Becomes a Home

The morning's first pale rays shone through the opening to the hollow in which Colwyn slept. The warmth tickled his eyelids, bidding him to wake. In those first seconds of wakefulness, he failed to recognise his surroundings, and alarm raced through him. Then, remembering the events of the previous afternoon, he saw he was sleeping in his new home. In quick succession came another memory—or, an impression really, rather than a clear memory—of a dream. It was a dream of hope and calm, a sense that all would be well.

The animals of the community had welcomed him, and the mice, Thomas and Meg, suggested he take up residence in this hollow, a short walk from their home in a hedge. The opening was a few feet up an impressive oak tree, not too high to easily climb to but high enough for safety. It gave him a lovely view of the meadow and forest beyond. As the rising sun revealed, the opening happily faced east.

Looking around him, Colwyn appreciated what he saw. All in all, this should be perfect. It probably would be if only I didn't miss my family so very much. Despite the soothing dream, now that he was fully awake, fear and doubt dragged his thoughts in a downward spiral. Maybe I should have stayed home and worked on my bad behavior. Did I really have to give up everything I've ever known? Can I really make a life here? And, despite the cheerful sunbeams dancing around the hollow, his gloom would surely have intensified if four little ears hadn't appeared at the bottom of his hollow's opening. Then there were four little eyes.

"He's awake" pronounced Sophie in a quiet indoor voice.

"Oh, goody! He's awake!" shrieked Carmen.

Before Colwyn knew it, two little mice were climbing all over him, talking so fast, and both at the same time, that he couldn't understand a thing they were saying. But one thing was perfectly clear—they were very excited to see him!

16

"Good morning, girls!"

Sophie exclaimed, "Oh, Colwyn, we're so happy to see you! We would have been here sooner, but mum made us wait till dawn."

Carmen continued, "We brought you breakfast, then we'll have the most best day ever!"

Then Sophie. "We'll take you all 'round the community and show you where everybody lives. That's important, you know!"

Back to Carmen. "And then we'll gather blackberries for afternoon tea with mum and dad."

A laughing Colwyn held up a paw. "Yes, that sounds great! Meanwhile, I smell something luscious. What's in the basket?"

In their excitement, the girls had forgotten all about it. But now, with a dramatic flourish, Sophie pulled away the cloth that covered half a dozen cream scones and a covered dish of lemon curd. Without further delay, all three eagerly selected a plump scone.

"Did your mum make these?" Colwyn asked, licking crumbs from his muzzle.

"Oh, yes," said Sophie, "she's quite good at it. We have several talented bakers here in the community, as you'll see."

"Well! I'm certainly looking forward to that!" He topped what remained of his scone with a generous dollop of lemon curd and smacked his lips in anticipation. "The scones have quite a tender crumb. I must remember to compliment Meg when I see her."

"And so you shall, at tea this afternoon! If you can come, that is," Sophie added, remembering her manners.

Colwyn replied with a gracious nod of his head. "I'd love to!"

Breakfast finished, Colwyn told the girls he'd need a few moments to get ready for the adventures they proposed.

"Why don't you two scamper back home with your basket? Tell me how to get to your hedge and I'll join you shortly."

to Colwyn's home village of Hawthorne

the benign woods

hazelnut copse

oak woods

Rosebud Cottage

Littleton Hedge

Littleton Community Center

Colwyn's tree

THE ANIMAL COMMUNITY

bank

Sweetbrier Sett

Ivy Knoll

Inn

to the Old Road

to the
deep
forest

the ancient oak

the Norman
tower

BEHIND

MILKWEED

MANOR

trash
heap

the
Mercantile

lawn and
gardens of
Milkweed
Manor

rock
wall

manor house →

manor village →

The girls gave him directions, then happily skipped off, swinging the now empty basket between them.

That's what I needed—a bit of diversion, a tasty breakfast, and the prospect of a fun day with entertaining company. He opened his pack, located his Sunday-best tunic, and slipped it on. He smoothed his fine grey-brown fur and combed his fingers through his luxurious whiskers. Finally, he checked his tail for burrs. Then, scrambling down the tree trunk, he headed towards the mice's hedge. He was actually whistling! *What do you know!*

* * * * *

That evening, Colwyn sat in the opening of his hollow watching the splendid sunset and smiling at memories of his day.

Just as they promised, Sophie and Carmen had guided their new friend all through the community, familiarizing him with the lay of the land and the locations of all the animals' homes. A few were out when they called, but everywhere else the residents happily greeted Colwyn and the mice. He felt welcome indeed and even received several invitations for dinner later in the week. By the end of the day, his social calendar was full! His only problem would be keeping all the invitations straight. How nice to be an independent young adult—which was how he was coming to view himself—memorizing dinner invitations rather than multiplication tables and the capitals of Europe!

Then there had been tea with Thomas, Meg, and the girls—a treat in many ways. The food was delicious, and the conversation was as delightful as the repast! They shared stories, and the girls, who were on their best behavior on this special occasion, contributed a few silly jokes. Colwyn did, however, need to correct the impression that he was an oversized mouse. He explained he was a rat, and that rats and mice, though different in many ways, notably size, were alike in many more.

As Colwyn prepared to depart, Meg, being a domestic sort of mouse, offered a few suggestions to help him settle into his hollow. Particularly, she thought decorating was of the highest importance and, indeed, the charms of her home testified to her devotion to all the domestic arts.

As it happened, Roxanne had expressed a similar view when he and the girls visited the Mercantile on their rounds through the community. Roxanne had given him a housewarming gift. It was a tiny ceramic figurine of a rat. The raccoon explained that it was a collectible, one of several different little ceramic animals the purveyor used to tuck into each box of Princess' Pride tea. She had several examples—a polar bear, an otter, a rooster, and so many more—but thought the rat clearly the most appropriate gift for Colwyn. Also, she had more than one of the rats, so its loss wouldn't diminish her own collection in any appreciable way. Roxanne, though a generous and thoughtful creature, had a strong attachment to her belongings!

Enjoying the memories of his day, Colwyn extracted the figurine from his pocket and studied it carefully. Yes, it was very nice—a careful and accurate representation of his species. He looked around the hollow for an appropriate spot for it but, since he had no furnishings, was at a loss. Finally, he put it on the floor in a corner where it should be safe.

Having spent the day out and about, he hadn't yet had an opportunity to unpack his sack. He was nervous about the task, fearing it would trigger another bout of sadness. Nonetheless, it needed to be done.

Come here, sack! Let's get on with it! He didn't have many belongings, so it didn't take long but, as predicted, it was an emotional experience.

The first items he drew from the sack were two everyday tunics, one light green and the other a pale blue. Of course, a rat's lifestyle being what it is, both were soiled and had been mended many times. Looking around the hollow, he spotted three small irregularities in the walls that would serve as makeshift pegs. Hanging the two from the pack, he then shed the one he was wearing and hung it up too. *There! Good job!*

Next was his seashell. Mama had given one to each of her children on the occasion of his or her one-month birthday. Mama's seashells were her pride and joy. They had been carefully handed down through the family as a proud testament to her ancestors' lives as sea rats. He held the seashell in his paws, warming it and drawing happy memories from it. That one-month birthday had been so special! Despite the tears stinging his eyes, he made a valiant effort to focus on the happy memory and feel gratitude for having this memento. *I'll put it next to the figurine for now.*

By far the largest item in his sack was a quilt. His grandmum made it for him to celebrate his birth, and he had slept with it his whole life. The pattern was amazingly intricate. "Starry Night," she'd called it. It was mesmerizing, with all the tiny patches of beautiful sky colors setting off the white stars. The stitches were tiny and even. He smiled as he remembered how proud his grandmum had been of her needleworking skills.

By far the largest item in the sack was a quilt.

She joyfully practiced the needle arts her whole life. This was interesting to Colwyn, as she had often told him her chore as a young girl was to knit socks for her entire, very large family. As a consequence, she spent her childhood knitting. She knitted while reading her lessons. She knitted while waiting for the school bus. She knitted during church sermons! She even knitted while waiting her turn at jump-rope. When her turn came, she'd put the knitting down and jump. Then, her turn over, she'd take the knitting right back up. You'd think, after all that knitting, as soon as she no longer had to, she'd never pick up a knitting needle—or any other kind of needle—again. But she loved it all her life! Colwyn smiled at the memory and envisioned her happily knitting socks for all the angels.

He had been so tired last night that he just fell asleep on the grass spread over the floor of the hollow, but tonight would be different. He carefully smoothed the quilt over the grass mattress. Now I have a proper bed—mattress and quilt!

Finished with the sack, he began folding it, but realised it wasn't quite empty. Feeling around in the bottom of the sack, he found a pebble, a pebble he was surprised to have forgotten. He'd found it—such a pretty thing—on the shore of Belisama's lake. It was perfectly smooth, a translucent pale aqua, and seemed to glow with an inner light. As he held it in his paw, he felt peaceful and calm. Perhaps the pebble has mystical power. It wouldn't surprise me! He held it for a few more moments, then set it with the seashell and figurine. *These three objects are important. My past, my future, and the promise.*

With that thought, he sat on his quilt, looking out the hollow opening for a while. As the sun set and twilight deepened, he suddenly felt very tired. He crawled between the quilt and grasses and wriggled into a comfortable position. It felt like being in his grandmum's arms, one of his most favorite places ever. His eyelids grew steadily heavier. The last thing he saw before slipping into a sound sleep was miraculous. He saw a shooting star.

* * * * *

The next morning, clouds covered the sky from the meadow to the forest beyond. Looks like rain! *I like the rain, as long as it's not too stormy.* A few moments later it did, in fact, start raining. The rat found the pattering of the drops falling on the tree leaves irresistibly soothing. *Think I'll have a little lie in!* It didn't take long to drift back to sleep.

Late that afternoon, Colwyn once again dressed in his best tunic and groomed himself. He'd been invited to Rosebud Cottage for dinner with the squirrel family. As he made the journey to the massive beech tree which housed the cottage, he couldn't help but admire his surroundings. The rain had stopped around noon. The sun was still *in absentia*, but the dampness clinging to everything had a charm of its own. It softened all sound. Footfalls were barely audible. Birds were singing, but their music was subdued. Animals moving through the undergrowth made little noise as they pushed aside moisture-softened foliage. Water drops clung to the edges of the leaves, occasionally falling to the ground with soft plopping sounds.

Soon he arrived at the tidy little home. The inhabitants clearly valued horticulture, as evidenced by the profusion of carefully tended plants in the nearby garden and the fragrant wreath of dried flowers and herbs which graced the door.

Just as Colwyn reached for the knocker, the door opened and there were the squirrels—Emma and her daughters Effie and Lily—smiling a warm welcome.

"Colwyn, come in, come in! Welcome to our home!" The girls gave Colwyn hugs, and Emma extended her paw as he entered the foyer. "Let me give you a quick tour."

The home was ingeniously laid out. The main living areas occupied connected hollows in the massive beech trunk, while leafy sleeping areas nestled in the branches above. They finished the tour in the living room. It was the coziest room he'd ever seen, with a bright fire crackling in the fireplace and inviting soft chairs gathered round it.

Above the fireplace, the entire wall was covered—crowded actually—with family portraits: squirrels of various generations, as evidenced by their clothing styles. An ornate stand held an ancient book with a beautifully tooled leather cover.

Emma noticed Colwyn studying the paintings. "Our family goes back a long way in this valley, Colwyn. The family bible here lists twenty-one generations, and I wouldn't be surprised if we go back even further. That portrait is my great-grandfather Winston, and next to him is my great-grandmama Victoria. I owe my treasured family recipes to her. She compiled many from earlier times, and those of us who came after added to the collection from time to time. Her own recipes, however, comprise the bulk of the collection."

"Such a rich history, Emma! I don't know much about my own heritage, except to say that although I was born beneath the apothecary shop in Hawthorne Village, our more distant heritage is a sea-faring one."

Sitting down to dinner, Emma proudly served one of the family's favorite meals: oven roasted acorns with corn compote and pickled beet greens. "Courtesy of great-grandmama's recipes!" She declared, then continued in another vein. "We're very happy to have you here, Colwyn."

"And I'm happy to be here, Emma! Everything smells utterly scrumptious."

"Thank you. But actually, I meant more than that. You're beginning a new chapter of your life, and we're happy that it's here, in this community. There can be so much excitement in a new beginning."

"I've certainly enjoyed a heart-warming welcome here, and I know I'll have a happy life with all of you. But I must say that beginning anew, exciting as it may well be, has its challenges. Truth be told, I'm rather at a loss. I need to build my life and, along with it, my place in this community. Yet I don't know how."

Concern wrinkled his brow, but he quickly recovered himself and focused on the lovely dinner and engaging company. As they enjoyed the repast, conversation ebbed and flowed. Sometimes the children took the lead, telling funny stories and describing their adventures around the community. Seeing the world through the innocent eyes of the young was delightful. At other times, the conversation settled on more adult topics with the girls listening politely, taking in what they could.

* * * * *

Later, when Colwyn thought back on their conversation, he found himself repeatedly returning to something Emma had said. "Colwyn, I'm sure with your special talents and interests you'll find a unique and valuable place in this community. I can't wait to see whom you become."

He never thought of himself as having talents or interests, at least not of a positive sort. After Papa disappeared, he found himself good at causing trouble. *Of course, that's not a talent to be proud of, nor does it have any place here!* He must find the positive in himself and apply it to making a difference in his own life and in the life of this community. He must think back to the days when his family was whole. What was good in him then? He remembered how much he loved his little brothers and sisters and how he liked to help everyone. He thought deep down, he had a good heart. That was something. Was it enough?

* * * * *

Emily proudly served one of the family's favorite meals.

Colwyn soon settled into a routine. He began the day with a visit to the mouse family, followed by a walk about, often accompanied by Sophie and Carmen. A bit of pottering about the place occupied the typical afternoon. He worked at getting things in order and making small improvements to his hollow, as a result of which it was becoming ever more serviceable and comfortable.

This afternoon he would be visiting Aunt Audrey at Sweetbrier Sett. He had met the badgers a few times and was eager to get to know them better. He knew there was a berry patch along the way, so he allowed extra time to stop and gather some fruit to share with his new friends.

* * * * *

"Colwyn, berries! You brought berries! How wonderful! Come in. I'll give you a tour of the sett, and then we can relax here on the patio and enjoy the sunshine and afternoon breezes and this lovely treat."

The sett was a marvel of underground engineering. It was a plethora of connected chambers—there were living chambers, dining chambers, storage chambers, and sleeping chambers. Everything one could need was here, snug and safe underground. Colwyn was particularly impressed with the neat piles of grass in the sleeping areas, as well as the ample supply of fresh bedding in storage. *Badgers are certainly clean animals. And accomplished excavators!*

Just outside the door, the patio was surrounded by lush ferns. "Colwyn, it's just you and I as Gwen and the twins are at the Inn. Evie needed help with the garden, so I volunteered them. You see, I'm always on the lookout for ways to develop civic responsibility in the youngsters. The twins, especially, are at the age where all they want to do is have fun! And days filled with nothing but fun can lead to trouble."

"How well I understand the pitfalls of youth! I'm afraid I didn't make a very good job of mine, or at least parts of it." Colwyn surprised himself at how much he revealed. But Aunt Audrey had a special quality which encouraged others to open up to her. Before he knew it, he was telling her all about what happened after losing his papa—the hard times he'd had and bad decisions he'd made.

"Colwyn, let's climb this little bank and sit on the grass. There's a lovely view of the valley from there," Audrey suggested, clearly with a purpose beyond enjoying the view. "Isn't it beautiful here? So magnificent yet calming at the same time. I often come here when I'm feeling sad, or lonely, or when I'm trying to solve a problem." After a pause, she added, "I sense that you're feeling all those things."

Colwyn's chin slumped to his chest. "You're right. I miss my family so much. This is a lovely, warm, welcoming community, but the fact is, I'm alone. Maybe I made a mistake coming here. How could I have thought I could just relocate and begin again, no problem? I don't know what to do, Audrey."

Audrey shifted to a more comfortable position and looked into Colwyn's eyes. "I understand, Colwyn. Let me tell you a story. Perhaps it will help in some way.

"The children and I are newcomers to this community—like you. And just like you, we came after a tragic loss. We used to live in a large sett quite a way from here. Several extended families lived together. We were happy and, we thought, safe. There were dozens of badgers in that sett. And my own family was quite large. I was the oldest child, followed by my sister Gillian, who was Arthur and Percival's mother. We also had several younger siblings who didn't yet have families of their own. Times there were happy, Colwyn, especially at the holidays. But the loss to come was so horrific that now I can't enjoy even the happy memories. It's as though I lost my past along with everything else."

Colwyn stayed still and quiet, wondering what he would hear next.

"One night, soon after we had all fallen asleep, there was a deadly raid. A 'cull,' as humans call it. We badgers have some friends in the human tribe, but also some terrible enemies who hate us and want a world without any of our kind. These haters organize secret nighttime attacks. They use shovels and dogs to dig us from our burrows, then mercilessly kill as many of us as they can. Young, old, weak, strong, it doesn't matter.

"My sister, mother, father, and all my other siblings lost their precious lives that night. I barely escaped with little Gwen, who was a babe in arms at the time, and my poor dear orphaned nephews. After a journey that I barely remember, we made our way here and began our own little sett. Hopefully we can live here in peace and escape the notice of humans."

"Oh, Audrey, that's awful. There are no words for how sorry I am."

They were both quiet for a while, Audrey mourning her family members, and Colwyn overcome with sorrow at the story of her loss.

After a while, Colwyn shared a very personal thought. "You know, I used to think it was my fault Papa didn't come home that horrible night. But lately, Audrey, I've wondered if he died at the hands of humans. Mama said he would never abandon us. And I know most of the humans in Hawthorne village—that's the human village I grew up in—didn't like us rats at all. But murder? I just don't know."

"It's possible, Colwyn." Audrey said gently. "What's not possible is that your papa not returning that night was your fault."

Colwyn considered that for a bit, then turned his thoughts back to Audrey and continued, speaking softly and respectfully. "How long have you been here, Audrey? And how are you now?"

"You know, I'm not even sure exactly how long we've been here. The early days are a blur. But it's been a while, Colwyn, since Gwen was a mere babe when we arrived. Beginning a new life isn't easy, or quick. But it's possible. Especially here."

"Despite everything, Audrey, at least you had Gwen and the boys, and thank God for it. You weren't alone!"

"No. Not like you, though there were many times when I felt alone, and totally without the strength to go on. But the life force, Colwyn, is strong. Maybe it's the strongest thing there is. In the end, I was strong enough, and so will you be. And even though you don't have family here—or maybe I should say you don't have family here yet—you're surrounded by animals who welcome you with all their hearts.

"Give us a chance, Colwyn, to be your new family. And let me give you a bit of advice. Don't isolate yourself. Get out and see one of us each and every day. Get to know us and let us get to know you. Not every day will be better than the last. There will be setbacks, yes, but things will get better in time. Happiness will come in a thousand little ways, including ways you can't possibly predict."

* * * * *

That night, warm and safe in his grandmum's quilt, watching the stars sparkle in the purple night, he thought long and hard about what Audrey had said. What a gift her words had been. He felt the seed of determination sprouting within him. *I can do this! I'll be fine.* He spent the night in a healing sleep filled with dreams of hope.

The next morning dawned exceptionally bright and beautiful. Colwyn awoke a new rat, eager for the day. As was his habit, he went to the opening of his hollow and looked all around, checking things out.

What's that? There was something strange on the ground at the base of his tree. True to his rat nature, he was reluctant to approach the unknown object, but curiosity soon got the best of him, and down he climbed. He found a small basket covered with a soft pink blanket.

foundling,
heritage
unknown

ITSY

Cautiously, he folded back the blanket to reveal...a tiny creature! It had a sharp nose with curious whiskers twitching non-stop, small round ears, and two bright eyes gazing directly into his. The creature squeaked softly. Colwyn couldn't help himself. Instinctively, he lifted the little mouse and cradled her in his arms. "What an itsy-bitsy thing you are! And the brightest eyes I've ever seen. Whoever you are, I'm instantly, hopelessly in love with you!"

Just then, Meg called out. "What do you have there, Colwyn?"

"Come and see!"

Seeing the baby mouse cradled in Colwyn's arms, Meg reached out to touch her. But the little thing squeaked a clear warning. She wanted to stay exactly where she was!

Soon Thomas, Sophie, and Carmen came to see what was happening.

"Oh, a baby! She's so cute," Sophie cooed, reaching towards her.

Once again, the baby squealed a warning.

"I don't think she wants anyone but you, Colwyn! I think you're a dad!" All the mice smiled. "But, seriously, we'd be happy to adopt this little foundling, and I know with time she'd come around and be a part of our mouse family."

"I'll call her Itsy!"

Colwyn's eyes hadn't left the little one. "Thank you, Meg. But if it's all the same to you, I'd like her to be my family. I'll name her Itsy."

When Nature unleashes her fury, the forces she
commands are strong beyond comprehension.
But they are neutral, being neither for nor
against the well-being of any individual creature.
The Life force is also strong and has the
advantage of taking a side—its own.

In Which the Mouse Family gets a New Home

Longer than anyone knew, Milkweed Manor has been standing in this valley at the edge of deep forest and overlooking verdant meadows. Saxon and Medieval chronicles make five mentions of the manor, all of them telling of the destruction of the house, usually by fire, and its subsequent reconstruction. Throughout its known history, the same family held it. Though that noble family had been more fortunate than most in its long, uninterrupted tenure of the property, its fortunes, as is usually the case, rose and fell over time. When Colwyn joined the animal community behind the manor house, the reclusive final lord Grimsley oversaw a much run-down property with a barely adequate staff of a groundskeeper, cook, and scullery maid.

There was another structure on the grounds, far older than the manor house and a fair distance from it—the ruin of a nine-hundred-year-old Norman stone tower. The south wall and part of the east and west walls had crumbled, but there was a strong tall corner still standing. A pair of crows, the community's guardians, made their home in that corner.

The duties and skills of guardianship had passed through countless generations of proud birds. The current guardians, Rupert and Rose, when perched atop the ancient tower, had a clear view of the width of the forest and the depth of the valley and well knew how to read the moods of the sky, the woods, the meadows, the lakes, and the streams.

What the pair read that night was ominous. A storm was coming, and it promised to be worse than the community had witnessed in a very long time. The crows sounded the alarm with a long series of loud jarring caws. The warning would carry a long way from the tower, but not far enough. Rupert and Rose lifted into the darkening sky. To be sure their warning reached everyone, Rupert circled to the west and Rose to the east, cawing until the entire valley knew, or at least should know, of the coming danger.

* * * * *

In their leaf and twig nest in the hedge, the mouse family was settling down for the night. They curled together in a warm cozy ball of fur. Their breathing deepened as the comfort of lying close together eased them towards sleep. When the warning came, they woke immediately, frightened by loud sounds—scary noises the youngsters had never heard before—and pressed more closely together.

It had been a long time since either mum or dad had heard such a warning, but they understood it immediately. A storm was coming, but more than that, a storm so strong that it threatened their very lives! Drawing the children even closer, Thomas and Meg conferred quietly but urgently. "We must go to Colwyn's hollow!" Thomas said.

Meg agreed. She explained the plan to the children, helped them into their jackets, then led them to the door. "Yes, it will be safer there. Everyone hold paws and don't let go no matter what! The most important thing is to stay together!" They formed a chain, firmly clasping paws, with the children, Sophie and Carmen, between the two adults.

"I'm scared!" squeaked Carmen, and Sophie immediately squealed "Me too!"

The winds were growing stronger by the minute. Even large branches were straining and creaking. The mouse children, their eyes wide with fright, clung to each other. The fearful little group hesitated at their doorway, but the parents knew the longer they waited the more hazardous their short journey would be. Saying a silent prayer, they pulled the children into the storm and hurried towards Colwyn's sheltered hollow a few feet up a nearby tree.

* * * * *

Feeling safe in his hollow and ensuring Itsy was sleeping peacefully, Colwyn's thoughts turned to the mouse family. He was afraid for them in their vulnerable nest, so he determined to bring them to his hollow for safety. Rushing into the storm, he intercepted them not far from their nest. "Hurry!" He quickly turned to lead the way. As they scrambled up the tree trunk, the storm's first peel of thunder boomed in the distance.

"Eeeek!" screamed the mice as they dove into the hollow. The noise woke Itsy, who added her squeals to the melee. All three children were shivering with cold and fear.

"Sophie, Carmen, let's get you warm and dry," Meg urged, and wrapped each of them in a blanket. "Poor babies! Come snuggle." Colwyn gently placed Itsy on her blankie, folded it snugly round her, and placed the swaddled mouse in Meg's arms with the other children. She sat holding the precious bundles and sang a soothing lullaby. Soon, the little ones were calmly dozing, and it wasn't long before Meg joined them.

Thomas and Colwyn stood in the opening of the hollow, watching the storm close in. Colwyn had been in the community for several months now, and he and the mouse family had become quite close. Little Itsy's arrival brought them even closer. The storm was the first real danger they would face together.

I think we're safe, but I have a bad feeling about this storm. Each had the same foreboding.

* * * * *

At Rosebud Cottage, the first alarm sent Emma and her girls, Effie and Lily, rushing to prepare for the coming storm. "You know what to do, girls! Let's get to it," Emma urged, and they rushed outside. Emma secured the shutters on Rosebud Cottage while the girls brought the pots of precious herbs indoors.

Lily could carry a few of the smaller ones, Effie hefted the middle-sized ones, but it took both to move the largest. "These stupid pots are so heavy," Lily complained.

"Yes, but these herbs are precious," Effie reminded her younger sister. "You seem to think highly enough of them when Mama bakes her fiddlehead fern and mushroom pie! Imagine you're enjoying a slice of that pie and maybe the pots will seem lighter!"

Just as they finished moving all the pots, the weather quickly took a turn for the worse. The grey drizzle escalated to a pelting rain. Emma sent the girls inside to begin drying off while she remained outdoors stacking extra firewood on the porch. Even though she held her fluffy tail above her head like an umbrella, she was soon drenched. Finished with her storm preparations, she shook herself off, went inside, and lit the fire that was already laid in the fireplace. The family soon had a crackling fire. They would be sleeping downstairs tonight—far safer than their leafy sleeping chambers! Emma made chamomile tea for herself and hot chocolate for the girls. They all snuggled in their warmest blankets and settled by the fireplace for a long, perhaps sleepless, night.

* * * * *

The girls brought the pots of precious herbs indoors.

At Sweetbrier Sett, the badgers' underground home, Aunt Audrey's response to the crows' alarm was to amble out the mouth of the den. She found a comfortable patch of grass and sat down, ready to watch the storm come in. She knew that storms could be dangerous—in fact, she feared for some of her friends in the community—but she found storms beautifully fascinating, nonetheless. She would stay outside as long as she could but would not be reckless. After all, her daughter and nephews depended on her. Seeing the threatening darkness smudge the horizon, then climb relentlessly upward until it covered the whole the sky was just so exciting! She loved storms! She was a scientist at heart, and wished she knew more about them. *Where do they come from? What causes them? What is their purpose in the scheme of things?*

As she studied the sky, she reflected, *I've seen so many storms, especially where I used to live, but our setts were never damaged.* The only natural threat would be flooding, but the careful layout of their chambers and tunnels minimized that possibility. It would take deep water standing across the whole forest to flood the sett—something that had never, in living memory or even in legend, happened. The sett was ready.

As always, there was a ready supply of clean grass in the storage chamber. They would have fluffy fresh bedding for a comfortable night. And tucked away underground, they probably wouldn't even hear the storm rage.

* * * * *

Nearby, Roxanne lived in an elaborate structure she had cleverly constructed in an ancient oak. The tree's lower trunk had acquired natural hollow chambers over the centuries, and the raccoon had painstakingly converted them. Her mercantile occupied the ground floor. Just outside the door was a porch onto which, in good weather, she could expand her display of tempting items. Her living quarters, as well as storage areas, occupied the upper levels. When Rose and Rupert sounded their raucous alarm, Roxanne didn't even notice! An avid collector, she was thoroughly absorbed with inspecting, admiring, cleaning, and cataloging her latest finds from the manor trash heap. Fortunately, given its construction, her home was secure from the coming storm—throughout which Roxanne remained totally unaware!

* * * * *

The Inn at Ivy Knoll stood in a clearing in the forest. It was a small stone building with a slate roof. Rumor had it a long-ago lord had it built as a playhouse for the children of the manor. It was clearly old, as ivy nearly encased it. The proud little structure had already weathered countless storms and still stood strong!

Audrey found storms beautifully fascinationg.

Three brown hares lived at the inn: the elderly Glenna and Graham, and their youngest daughter, Evie. The building itself was solid, but since storm preparation tasks fell solely to her, Evie had worked over the years to minimize them. *I'm so glad I installed these new storm sashes and latches.* As she worked, the rising wind twisted her coat around her. The rain caught on her eyelashes, making it nearly impossible to see. Shaking her head in an attempt to clear her vision, she almost caught one of her long ears as she slammed a sash shut. *That would have hurt. Really bad!* She finished securing the sashes, then rushed inside. Just as she bolted the door behind her, lightning flashed across the sky, illuminating everything with an eerie white light.

Indoors, the sudden light revealed a tender sight. Her parents were snoozing comfortably, settled in their chairs in front of the fire with blankets over their laps. Evie smiled and kissed each of them gently on the cheek. They had safely weathered many storms in their long lives and apparently felt no concern over this one!

Evie sank into an overstuffed chair that was more comfortable than stylish and spread an old Victorian crazy quilt over her lap. She closed her eyes and sat quietly for a while, thinking of her friends living in less secure homes, especially the mouse family. She said a prayer for each of them. *Comfort them and keep them safe!* A loud clap of thunder—which her parents slept peacefully through—startled her and interrupted her thoughts. A novel, a historical romance by one of her favorite authors, waited on the table beside her. Prepared for a long night, she opened the book and began reading.

* * * * *

The wind rose to a howl. The wildly swaying trees moaned and groaned. Throughout the forest, mighty branches and even whole trees surrendered to the storm, crashing to the ground, the sound rivalling thunder. The pelting rain turned to hail that stung and ripped everything in its path. Then the rains returned, heavier than ever. The strong gusts drove the raindrops sideways. Thunder boomed. Every bolt of lightning, like a camera flash, briefly lit the destruction, evidence of the storm's fury.

After several hours, the lightning and thunder slowly subsided, then stopped. The drenching rains settled to showers and eventually to a light drizzle. When the first dim light of dawn finally came, it revealed a ravaged landscape littered with fallen trees, drifts of leaves torn from their branches, and twisted, broken limbs. The birds who should have been greeting the new day were silent, or, perhaps, their songs were muffled by the wind noisily shifting the storm debris. Shortly, the wind calmed. The weak remnants of the storm were moving west, and the sun was now fully visible in a narrow band of blue sky at the eastern horizon. Rupert and Rose cawed the "all clear."

The badgers were the first to emerge from their shelter. As Audrey expected, the sett had sailed through the storm undamaged. But she guessed that others had not been so fortunate. Rested from a good night's sleep, she and the youngsters set out to help wherever they were needed.

At the inn, the hares were sitting around the table enjoying their breakfast and reliving past storms. Evie had been up at dawn assessing damage. As for the inn itself, the only problem was a few slates blown from the roof. They could easily be replaced. Her beloved garden, though, was a different story. The hail had tattered the plants. The wind had tossed branches, leaves, and flower heads over the paths, flowerbeds, and lawns. The climbing rose, the gorgeous iconic sight that greeted everyone who visited the inn, still clung to its arch, but the storm had stripped away many of the leaves and flowers. And the iron arch itself was twisted and tilting. The tattered plants would recover in time. The strewn debris would be a difficult but manageable clean-up task. As for the arch, well, Evie didn't know what to do about that!

* * * * *

Emma stood in the doorway at Rosebud Cottage surveying the grounds. *I'm so glad we brought the herbs indoors!* The pots had been spared the near ruin that the wind and hail wreaked on the rest of the garden. The squirrel stepped outside to tour the damage, but snapped gnarled branches laying at odd angles made the footing tricky. Skeletal rose bushes seemed to reach out to her, their petals and leaves littering the garden paths. Tender blossoms lay crushed in the mud, snapped from their stems by the weight of the rain. She gasped in dismay at what she saw next. Her pride and joy, the honeysuckle hedge, looked like a vandal had attacked it with a giant eggbeater!

The damage overwhelmed her, and tears filled her eyes. *This should be the most beautiful time of year in the garden, but it's a wreck! It will take so much work—and so much time—to bring it back.* She didn't know if she had it in her. At least the herbs, the secret ingredient in her famous fiddlehead fern and mushroom pie, were safe.

* * * * *

The storm had done much damage throughout the valley. But of all the animals in the community, it was the mice who lost the most. At first light, Colwyn and Thomas crept to the opening in the hollow and fearfully peered out. Thomas' sense of foreboding from the previous night was unfortunately prescient. What they saw was horrifying. The ragged broken end of a huge branch protruded menacingly from the mice's hedge, now thoroughly crushed. Thomas felt an emptiness he had never felt before.

"We could have all been killed, Colwyn! We could have all been killed! Thank goodness for the crows, and for you! Sheltering here saved our lives!" The mouse slumped in the doorway, dreading the moment when his family would confront the tragedy that had befallen them as they slept.

Colwyn laid his paw on his friend's shoulder. "Your loss is terrible. Terrible! But what a blessing you and your family are safe." After a respectful pause, he added "And remember, Thomas, you have a whole community to support you."

The badgers soon arrived on the scene, finding the mouse family staring hopelessly at the destroyed hedge that yesterday had been home. "The crows told us! Oh, this is awful!" Aunt Audrey rushed to the mice and gathered them to her, comforting them as best she could. "You poor souls!" Meg and the children sobbed in Aunt Audrey's arms. Thomas stood wordlessly by. Colwyn looked away, silent tears staining his cheeks.

The squirrels had also correctly guessed that the little mouse house would be vulnerable to the ravages of the storm, and soon they too arrived, ready to help in any way they could. For their part, the squirrel and badger children gently moved the young mice away from the distressing scene and began to entertain them with simple games.

"Thomas, Meg, you have a lot of help for rebuilding!" Colwyn said encouragingly.

"Yes," Thomas replied hesitantly, "but where—and what? Truthfully, at the moment I can't help but wonder if the homes that we mice build are pure folly! Look how easily ours was destroyed."

Seeing Thomas in such distress wounded Meg's heart. *He's always been my rock, and now he's overwhelmed. I'm here for you, my dear Thomas.* "As far as 'where,'" Meg said, "I certainly couldn't live in any part of this hedge again. Just the sight of that big branch spearing the middle of it would scare me every day of my life."

"Agreed, Meg! Our new home has to be somewhere else—well out of sight of this hedge."

Audrey had an idea. "As far as what to build, Thomas, underground setts have kept us badgers safe from storms. Maybe you should consider a burrow. Many kinds of animals live in them." She paused to give that thought time to sink in.

Emma, thinking of her home—which was a combination of a hollow trunk and leaf sleeping chambers higher in the tree—made another suggestion. "What about a hybrid? Maybe a burrow under a hedge combined with a leaf and twig nest low in the branches above it."

Thomas was silent for some time, giving his friends' ideas careful thought. It was a struggle to set his emotions aside and approach the problem rationally, but that was what he simply had to do.

"Despite what I said before, I suppose there must be good reasons that we field mice have traditionally built our homes this way. Seeing this destruction, it may sound silly to say, but I still think it's true. After all, Nature does her best to care for all her creatures, and somehow this design suits mice. As for a repeat of this tragedy, I think it's unlikely. After all, last night's storm surely brought down all the weak branches."

Meg spoke up. "Thomas, I understand your points, and they make perfect sense. I'm just not sure, though, that I would ever feel safe again in a nest of just twigs and leaves." She paused and looked into Thomas' eyes. "I like the hybrid idea. It would be like the home we're used to, but with a storm cellar."

Thomas rubbed his chin and twitched his whiskers. "That could work, Meg. Most of the time we could live in the nest, just like before, but retreat to the burrow when we needed to. And maybe the burrow would be cooler on hot nights."

"Or warmer on cold nights," Meg added, glad that Thomas seemed to be warming to the idea. Her cheeks flushed, she shyly added, "I'd like a window. I've always wanted a window." *Perhaps it's too much to ask. I shouldn't be greedy. I must seem ungrateful for the help they're offering.* She felt a bit embarrassed.

"I don't see how a window would work in the burrow portion, but maybe in the upper part. What do you think, Thomas? Audrey? Emma?" said Colwyn and, noticing Meg's pink cheeks, he added, "I'm glad you spoke up about the window, Meg! We need to build you a new home that will be safe from storms, but also one you and your family will love! Anything else?"

"Yes," Meg answered shyly, grateful for her friend's compassion, "a door that we can decorate for the holidays! And I do so appreciate your asking."

"It's settled then! A hybrid with a door and a window," Colwyn said. "Thomas, Meg, of course you're welcome to stay with me until your new home is ready.

"What do all of you think about beginning the build tomorrow? I'd like to scout out some other hedges as possible sites—or maybe some of you know of good spots. In any case, I think it would be helpful for everyone to sleep on the question of how to build this hybrid structure. We'll meet here in the morning, finalize the plans, and get to work. What do you say?" The mice readily agreed, as did everyone else. So, the little crowd dispersed for the night.

* * * * *

The next morning dawned clear and warm. Everyone was back at Colwyn's home just after breakfast, fresh and eager to get started. After a bit of back and forth, they settled on their plan, then set out to look at three potential sites.

The first was a small hedge near a stream. The second was a larger hedge at the edge of a meadow. The third was a thick hedge in the forest. The mice chose the second. The stream was too noisy, and the forest was too scary. They liked the view of the meadow.

Once Thomas and Meg selected the exact spot in the hedge for the leaf and twig nest, the badger boys set about digging the burrow. Meanwhile, their sister Gwen and the squirrel girls, Effie and Lily, set off to gather materials. Just as they were returning with the first bundles, Roxanne arrived towing a large sack and wearing a broad, sly smile.

"Gather round, everyone," commanded the raccoon. "I have something very special here!" With that, she slowly and dramatically drew something from the sack— a gorgeous piece of etched glass in a soft rose color.

Meg squeaked "A window!"

But there was more! Roxanne reached into the sack again and produced a lovely small arched piece of walnut decorated with intricately carved cable molding, and...a crystal knob!

"A door! Oh, Roxanne, they're exquisite! Nothing could be better!" Her eyes were bright as she added, "Your kindness touches my heart." Truth be told, the decision to let go of her treasures had been difficult for Roxanne. But Meg's happiness made up, at least partially, for the pain of parting with her beloved possessions

Meg squeaked, "A window!"

Colwyn, being a relatively new arrival to the community and previously living beneath a shop where items were traded for bright coins, was a bit alarmed. "How will you be able to pay for those?" he whispered to Thomas.

To the young rat, Thomas' answer was remarkable. "We don't have money here, Colwyn. We help each other. So, you see, kindness is our currency."

"That's amazing, Thomas! Kindness as currency! Then we're certainly all very wealthy! I keep learning new and wonderful things about this community!"

Thanks to the work of many hands and hearts, the little house was finished mid-afternoon. Roxanne's gifts added touches of beauty and an air of elegance to the otherwise rustic structure. Thomas spoke for the whole mouse family in heartily thanking everyone who had helped.

"It's so beautiful," Meg exclaimed, close to tears—once again—with happiness.

"It's so strong," Thomas whispered, overcome with emotion.

"It's so fun!" the children squeaked!

Everyone was proud of the house they had built, the house that the mouse family would soon turn into a home!

"How I wish I could thank you all with a lovely tea party," Meg said, "but, sadly, I have nothing to share as everything is destroyed."

"Yes, you do!" It was Evie, the hare from The Inn at Ivy Knoll. She kissed Meg on the cheek and handed her a bulging basket covered with a daffodil yellow damask cloth. Evie hadn't ventured out yesterday after the storm. Instead, she'd stayed home taking care of the inn and her elderly parents. The crows stopped by to tell her about the mouse house destruction and rebuild, so she spent much of the day baking scones and preparing other delicacies.

Meg gratefully accepted Evie's gift. She spread the cloth on the ground by the hedge that was their new home, and, reaching into the basket, took out the makings of a most inviting tea party! There were Evie's signature carrot scones with lemon curd, fresh raspberries, tender fern fronds, and afternoon-blend tea in a fancy bone china teapot.

The day's hard work made big appetites, and big appetites made short work of Evie's delicious treats. Meg was thrilled to play hostess. Everyone enjoyed the conversation and fellowship. All those present that day, both those who had lost their home to the storm and those who helped rebuild it, were grateful to live in such a loving community as this one in the forest behind Milkweed Manor.

When times are darkest it seems that's the way
it will always be. We think we know how things
will play out. But we don't. Life has many
surprises for us. There are happy endings more
often than we appreciate.

In Which Thea is Found

The morning sunlight sparkled in the tiny dewdrops tipping every leaf along the path leading from Rosebud Cottage to the nearby woods. It lit the cheerful faces of the wildflowers as they opened to the new day and flashed off the ripples patterning the stream. This was the girls' favorite time, when everything came alive promising another glorious day. Effie and Lily, the squirrel children, each carried a basket as they headed to their special spot—a sunny little clearing filled with soft grass and shy violets and lined with graceful ferns. They planned to play for a while. After that, they would collect tender young fiddleheads, then continue into the woods beyond the clearing to collect mushrooms. Mama was going to make their favorite meal for dinner—her famous fiddlehead fern and mushroom pie, one of the many recipes in the old book handed down from the girls' great-great-grandmama. *Maybe tonight Mama will let me help with the crust!* Effie, the elder sister, thought gleefully.

As the girls strolled along the path, they chattered about what a fun adventure it would be collecting the ingredients for the pie. They greeted the birds singing in the trees and scratching in the leaves under the bushes. "Hello, little wrens! Aren't you singing pretty today!" Startled frogs jumped into the nearby stream as they passed, escaping imagined danger. And in turn, the startled frogs startled the little silvery fish who darted for cover. "Sorry, frogs! Sorry, fish!" the girls laughed. Butterflies and bumble bees were already busily collecting pollen, moving determinedly from flower to flower. The girls admired their industriousness and smiled, knowing it would be rewarded with honey. They hoped the bees would share a bit with them! As for the butterflies, they were pure delight for the eyes with the sun shining through their delicate iridescent wings.

The walk was lovely this morning, and the girls were almost to the clearing when a strange sound stopped them in their tracks. A sniffling sob came from a clump of ferns near the side of the path. "What's that?" Lily was alarmed.

Effie cautiously parted the fern fronds.

Effie exclaimed, "It sounds like sobbing, but what could make someone so sad on such a fine morning?" They stopped to listen more carefully and, sure enough, it really did sound like a creature trying unsuccessfully to choke back tears.

Effie cautiously parted the fern fronds. A bit of pink among the green leaves caught her attention, and when she looked more closely, she saw a tiny owl slumped in the foliage. Tears were pooling in those big round golden eyes and spilling down those feathered cheeks. It was this dear little bird who was crying! Remembering Mama's warnings about strangers, Lily held back. But Effie, emboldened by compassion, spoke to the pitiable creature.

"What's wrong, little friend? What could possibly be breaking your heart on this fine morning? Surely it can't be as bad as it seems!"

With great effort, the owlet choked back her tears and replied. "Yes, indeed it could be, and even worse as a matter of fact! Mum and all of us fledglings were sleeping peacefully in our nest when something scary happened. Mum said it was a 'storm.' There was hideous thunder and terrifying lightning. It was awful. But then it got much worse! The wind tore our nest—our home—to pieces! We all fell to the ground.

"I don't know what happened next, but when I woke, I was cold and wet and my beautiful pink bed jacket that mum made for me was torn and muddy. But most horrible of all, I was all alone, separated from my family." She paused for a good cry. "I've been wandering by myself ever since. I'm so sad. I'm—Oooooooo..."

Effie's heart broke to hear the plight of this sweet little creature. Betraying her nervousness, Lily flicked her fluffy tail side to side as she cautiously crept forward and asked the owlet her name.

"Thea," she whispered. "Mum said it's a special name. It means 'goddess' in ancient Greek. The goddess of wisdom had an owl as her companion. Mum was very learned and wise, of course." And at that, Thea's sobs deepened.

Earlier, Lily had been gathering violets. She gently placed the tiny bouquet in a buttonhole in the owlet's bed jacket. "They smell so good! You need something cheerful, even if it's just a little thing."

Effie and Lily wrapped their arms around Thea. "Cry it out, Thea. You've had a terrible time! Let the tears flow." As Thea wept, the squirrel sister's eyes met, and they knew what they would do. "Thea, come home with us! You can eat a lovely hot meal and sleep in a safe and cozy bed. I know that Mama would never forgive us if we didn't offer you the comforts with which we ourselves are blessed."

Thea rallied, just a bit, and the squirrels, each walking on one side of the owlet and tenderly supporting a little wing, led the foundling back to Rosebud Cottage.

* * * * *

Emma was busy in the kitchen when, through the window, she saw her girls coming up the path supporting something between them. Moving to the doorway to meet the trio, she saw it was a little owl—an owlet in pitiful condition indeed!

"Mama, this is Thea. We found her in the woods!" Effie explained.

"Little darling, come in and rest. My goodness, your jacket is soaking wet! Let's get you into something dry and warm," Emma said, gently removing the torn and soiled garment. The jacket was made from delicate pink chenille and had lustrous heart-shaped mother-of-pearl buttons. She counted four buttons, but there had obviously been five. Though now dirty and torn, it must have once been very pretty.

"Did your mother make this for you, Thea?"

"Yes. It was so pretty, but now it's ruined!"

Emma tried to soothe her. "It's muddy and torn, but definitely not ruined. I'll wash and mend it for you, and it'll be nearly good as new."

At the mention of her mum, Thea began sobbing again. Emma wrapped her in a warm blanket, hugged her, and held her close. When the owlet quieted, Emma sat her gently in front of the fire and fetched an acorn tart and a cup of warm milk. "Try to eat and drink, little one. You need to build your strength."

As Thea nibbled on the tart and sipped the milk, she looked into the fire with wide sad eyes. *Oh, Mum! Where are you? Are you OK? I miss you so much! Will I ever, ever see you again?*

Just then, there was a knock at the door. "Colwyn!" Emma cried, opening the door. "Forgive me! With all the commotion I quite forgot I invited you for dinner. But come in! Come in!" She looked around curiously. "Where's Itsy?"

"She's with the mice family, having a sleepover. She, Sophie, and Carmen are very excited, but it's going to be a trying evening for Thomas and Meg, I'm afraid!" Stepping into the room, Colwyn saw the little owl wrapped in a blanket and staring into the fire. He gave Emma a questioning look.

"The girls found her in the forest," his hostess explained. "She was lost, cold, and hungry, separated from her family in the storm. Naturally they brought her home with them. Come meet our dear little guest, Thea—the poor soul."

Colwyn approached the owlet with quiet words of sympathy and encouragement and, sitting beside her, laid his paw on her shoulder. With his gentle manner and kindly, soothing voice, he had a gift for bringing comfort to others. "You're in good paws here, little one. These kind squirrels will take the best care of you." Then, turning towards his hostess, continued, "And, Emma, no matter about dinner. You have your hands full!"

"Thank you for being so understanding, Colwyn, but you will certainly join us for a meal. I'm afraid there won't be fiddlehead fern and mushroom pie tonight. I know I can put something tasty together though."

The squirrel girls were disappointed. They would not be having their favorite meal. Nonetheless, they pitched in and helped Mama make a nice dinner from last night's leftovers. Soon a savory acorn and corn porridge was steaming nicely. In fact, it smelled so delicious that everyone promptly forgot about the pie!

Emma was about to fill a bowl for the little owl when soft muffled sounds came from the living room. Investigating, she found Thea lying on her side in front of the fire, sound asleep and snoring quietly. She tucked a pillow under the owlet's head and gently adjusted the blanket. "She needs her sleep," she reasoned out loud, "A break from her worries will do her a lot of good."

As Colwyn, Emma, and the girls enjoyed their meal, they conversed quietly. The girls filled Colwyn in on all the details of Thea's misfortunes, and Colwyn related the recent goings-on with him and his friends, the mouse family. "It's beyond lovely to see such a sweet family settling into their new home after they lost their last in the storm. This is quite a community we live in—quite a blessing! As for Thea, it will be best, of course, to find her family—and we'll all do what we can to make that happen— but if she doesn't, she'll certainly have a happy life here."

Colwyn was a popular dinner guest with the squirrel family as well as with the hares, badgers, and mice. And this shared meal demonstrated why. He was gracious, kind, and caring. Such a change from that low point in his young life. He no longer needed to remind himself to behave well. It had become second nature.

* * * * *

The next morning, Effie and Lily's first thoughts were of Thea. "Let's see how she's doing," Lily excitedly urged Effie. They ran downstairs and there the little owl was, sitting in front of the fire rubbing the sleep from her eyes.

"Dear girl," Effie addressed the owlet. "How are you feeling this morning?"

She started off bravely enough. "I'm warm and safe and not alone. I'm very thankful for that." Then her voice faltered. "But I miss my family so much. I don't know how I'll ever find them. And they must be so worried about me! It's just awful!" She started to cry, and both squirrel girls put their arms around her, gazing sadly at each other as they comforted her.

Emma was just bringing breakfast to the table and witnessed the emotional scene. Sitting in front of Thea, she took her wing between her paws. "Thea, I know you're sad. Of course, you miss your family."

"Yes," Thea whimpered.

Emma continued. "You're too young to be on your own. But you're not! You're with us, and we will take care of you. Everyone in the community will be looking for your family." Thea stopped sobbing and looked trustingly into Emma's eyes. Emma gripped the little wing more tightly. "Meanwhile, it's fortunate that you're not hurt physically. Take each day as it comes and try to enjoy what good you find in it." She paused a moment. "And now, come have some breakfast."

Thea brightened a bit as she drank tea with honey and ate toast spread with butter and the most marvelous marmalade. Soon, conversation picked up, and the squirrel girls suggested it would be a perfect day to make a second try at the fiddlehead fern and mushroom hunt that had been interrupted the previous day. "What do you think, Thea? Are you up to it?"

"Well, as an owlet, I'm not very good at covering ground, but I'd like to try! It would do me good, I guess." And with that, she gave Emma a brave smile. "Can we go slow?" They all agreed that Thea would set the pace.

Late the previous evening after Colwyn left, Emma had cleaned and repaired Thea's pink bed jacket. She retrieved it from her sewing basket and helped the little owl slip it on. "I'm afraid it lost a button. I didn't have any as pretty as the ones your mum used. But I did find a heart-shaped button to replace the one that's lost."

"Thank you! I love this jacket so much. My mum made it for me..." I'll make the best of the day ahead—it's what Mum would want.

* * * * *

Emma watched the little trio set off—slowly—in the warming sunshine. Since Thea was still somewhat unsteady from her recent trauma, the squirrel girls walked on either side of her, ready to support her if she stumbled. This morning, they chose a different route than the one they had followed the day before. They didn't want to upset Thea by passing the place they had found her. Of course, they couldn't avoid that place forever, but today wasn't the day to stir bad memories that were lying barely beneath the surface.

On their way, they took special pains to bring cheerful sights and sounds to the owlet's attention. "Look, Thea! Isn't the sky the most beautiful color of blue? Cerulean, I think I'd call it!" Effie observed.

Then Lily, "Do you hear that sweet sound? It's a wren. They're such happy, perky little birds! My personal favorite! Oh, and look! It's a mouse running for cover in those ferns!" There was no end to wonderful things to see and hear in the forest.

And then, much to Lily's and Effie's delight, Thea joined in. "These violets are so pretty. If I gather some for your mama, do you think they'll droop before we get back?"

"That's so sweet! She'll love them! But why don't you pick them on our return?" Effie advised. "That way they'll go into a vase sooner!"

"Yes, that's a good idea!" As she imagined Emma's delight at receiving the pretty flowers, Thea's mood lifted.

They soon came to a small clearing. Wild mushrooms dotted the earth. "This is wonderful!" Lily exclaimed, pressing her paws together in an excited gesture. She and Effie patiently tutored the little owl in selecting the most tender and flavorful ones. As the birds chirped in the trees and the butterflies feasted in a nearby stand of milkweed, the trio worked quietly, each concentrating on her selections. It wasn't long before the mushroom basket was brimming over.

They didn't have to walk far before they came to another clearing, and wouldn't you know it—luck was with them. "Look!" Effie pointed. "Look! It's full of ferns!" Sure enough, the ground was carpeted with forest plants, including several vigorous clumps of ferns. Once again, the squirrels instructed Thea. "You only want the fiddleheads, fern fronds that are still tightly curled. And the lighter green, the better. If you see bug bites on one, just pass it by." Thea was a quick learner. Though she could clearly distinguish between ferns and other plants, for a joke she picked a dandelion leaf and slipped it into the basket. "Oops! Who put this in here?" Everyone had a good laugh.

This little joke of Thea's is such a good sign, thought Effie.

The hunt had proven quite successful even though the going, as predicted, was slow. With the baskets overflowing with mushrooms and fiddleheads, the girls headed back towards Rosebud Cottage. Along the way, Thea gathered violets for Emma. The sun was warm, the woods was alive with birds and butterflies, and the girls, quite pleased with themselves, were smiling ear to ear.

"Oh, good squirrel girls, good, good girls!" Effie heartily sang the first—and, as yet, only—line of a song, then nodded to Lily with a challenge to add the second line.

"Walking in the woods, the pretty, spring woods!" Lily added, then both the squirrels gestured dramatically to Thea—your turn!

"Met a little owl, a cute, sweet, owl!" Thea added.

Then, as inspiration struck, all three chimed, "Walking in the woods, the pretty, spring woods!" Grinning happily, they sang songs all the way home and would have skipped to the music if they could.

* * * * *

Hearing the happy song, Emma peered out the window. Well, well! This beautiful morning, companionship, and a little chore have conspired to lift Thea's spirits! It may not last long, but what a wonderful reprieve from her troubles. She stepped outside and waited for the girls, wiping her paws on her apron—she had been working on the pie crust.

Effie and Lily slowed their pace so Thea could press ahead with her violets. "Emma, I picked these for you! I hope you like them!"

"Oh, Thea," Emma smiled brightly at the little owl and gave her a kiss on her forehead, "they're beautiful - and they smell soooo good! Thank you, sweetie! I'll put them in my prettiest vase right away!" With her paw on Thea's shoulder, she turned her attention to the squirrel girls.

"Look at those baskets! You've all done a great job. Bring them on inside, then maybe you'd like to play a game before dinner."

"But, Mama, we want to help with the pie," Lily protested. "We want Thea to see how you make it."

"That's one good-looking pie!"

"Come on, then." Emma led the way and found aprons for all three. "Wash your paws—and wings!"

Emma was concerned that the domestic scene would remind Thea of her painful separation from her own family. Sure enough, Thea's large soulful eyes were shining with tears. Emma wrapped her arm around the foundling's shoulders. "I know, little one." She paused, allowing a few moments to pass, then gently added, "Come help with the pie."

While the girls tore the mushrooms and fern fronds into even sized pieces, Emma lined a pan with half of the crust and prepared her secret recipe sauce, the one with the precious herbs. The girls asked to stir the mushrooms and fern fronds into the sauce. "Carefully," Emma cautioned. "You don't want to bruise the mushrooms."

"Assembling the pie is next," Lily remarked knowingly to Thea. All three youngsters watched Emma pile a huge mound of the savory filling into the bottom crust, lay a second crust on top, carefully seal and crimp the edges, then pierce vent holes—which she arranged in a star pattern—in the top crust. She appreciated the way tiny details could make something special. Finally, she cut four mushroom shapes from crust scraps and patted them on the top crust for decoration. Stepping back, she put her paws on her hips and admired her work. "That's one good-looking pie!" Then into the oven!

A while later, all four were seated round the kitchen table enjoying the special meal. A perfect bake, Emma thought proudly.

"Sooooo good," enthused Lily.

"My absolute forever favorite!" exclaimed Effie.

"Never tasted anything like it!" Thea smiled. This would be an acquired taste, the little owl observed to herself.

* * * * *

A few days later, Emma decided to visit Evie, the young hare who lived at, and ran, the Inn at Ivy Knoll. It had been a while since she'd had a chat with her friend. And she planned to pick up a few of Evie's delicious carrot scones as a treat for the girls. Trading her apron for her favorite sky-blue shawl—she thought it brought out the brown in her eyes—she checked that the girls were safely occupied and counselled them against straying far from home. "I'll be back early afternoon in plenty of time for tea! Love you!"

"Love you more," all three girls responded, and Thea laughed.

It was a nice walk to the Inn, not too far but far enough to get the circulation going. Emma enjoyed the time alone, taking the opportunity to quietly ponder Thea's situation. *Such a sweetheart. A considerate, thankful guest. A delight to be around. I'm happy to have her with us as long as need be. But I'm worried—worried about her future.* In the long term, Emma knew Rosebud Cottage wouldn't be an appropriate home for an owl. Also, she had no way to teach her the life skills she would need. To complicate the situation even more, her girls were attached to Thea, and becoming more so with each passing day. When the owlet moved on, as seemed inevitable, there would be many sad faces, and probably dramatic declarations of broken hearts. But dramatic as the scene would be, she knew the hurt would be real.

A rose-covered arch marked the entrance to the Inn's garden, and as Emma walked through it, she was shocked to see it twisted and battered—presumably the work of the recent storm. At the same time, she realised she had been so preoccupied with her thoughts she had failed to notice any of her surroundings along the way. *I'm more worried about all the girls than I realised.*

"Emma! Emma! Over here!" Evie and Colwyn were waving at her from a table in the courtyard.

Emma and Evie hugged as Emma exclaimed, "Colwyn, what a nice surprise! And I see you're enjoying Evie's delicious pastries. Lovely!"

Evie fetched another place setting, poured tea for Emma, and passed the plate of treats. Emma took a chair, then selected a muffin bursting with walnuts! After her first bite, she enthusiastically complimented the baker.

"I have something I want to speak with you about, and, Colwyn, your wisdom on the subject will also be most welcome. But first, let's catch up!" After Emma expressed her shock at the state of the arch, the conversation centered on happier subjects for quite some time.

"So, Emma, what's on your mind?" Evie invited, and Emma poured out the thoughts that held her attention on her way to the inn. Evie and Colwyn both validated the squirrel's concerns, and after carefully considering the situation, Colwyn suggested getting the crows, Rupert and Rose, involved.

"Your point, Emma, about Thea needing to learn owl skills, is certainly a valid one," Colwyn agreed. "Of course, we don't know any owls other than the little one, but of all the animals in the community, I think Rose and Rupert would certainly be the best candidates to tutor her. You may remember that for a while, a pair of barn owls shared the old Norman tower with the crows. That was before my time here, but

I'm told the birds learned quite a bit about each other. In other words, the crows should be well versed in 'all things owl.' I'm sure they'd be happy to help. Why don't I contact them and bring them by as soon as they're available?"

* * * * *

And so, the lessons began. The crows were enthusiastic and energetic teachers. Since little Thea wasn't yet fully fledged, it was too soon for the all-important flight lessons. But there was so much else to learn, and Thea proved an apt pupil. First Rupert and Rose taught Thea about the importance of learning as much as she could about the world around her, and that knowledge would slowly ripen to wisdom—an owl's most important asset.

Next the lessons focused on owl heritage. "Owls, you know," Rose lectured, "were trusted companions of many of history's most fascinating creatures. One of the most famous was a Little Owl, an *athene noctuary* just like you, who was constantly at the side of the ancient Greek goddess of wisdom. Then there was Archimedes, a grey owl and the familiar of King Arthur's tutor, Merlin. The list goes on and on!"

Rupert continued, "Owls have always used their knowledge and wisdom to help animals in trouble. Because of their excellent sight—both physical and spiritual—you owls have traditionally been guides through dangerous places, showing the way of safety. Many creatures owe their very lives to the assistance of owls! Owls are also well-respected messengers between the animal and spirit worlds!"

Thea was feeling very proud to be an owl!

Rose taught Thea the importance of grooming. "Your remarkable feathers allow you to fly silently—a very important skill for gathering knowledge—but only if you keep them in top condition. You must clean them 'just so' each and every day!" Rose then gave Thea a demonstration, which would have been quite a comical sight for anyone who didn't know what she was doing!

Then there was nest-making. For these lessons, the crows accompanied Thea to the tower—it was a long walk, but necessary since Thea couldn't fly just yet. They stood in the center of the centuries-old Norman structure studying the ruins rising around them on the north, east, and south walls. Here and there, plants had taken root in the cracks between the stones, their stems cascading in lush green clumps.

"See how rough the surfaces are, how the stones are of different thicknesses? That means lots of shelves and cubbies, perfect for perches and nests. See the large ledge there? There's a nest on it. You can see some of its branches. That's the nest the barn owls abandoned a few years ago," Rupert explained.

He taught her how to choose the best places to build, places that would be sheltered from the weather, provide cover during the day, and give an excellent view of the surrounding territory.

"You'll need perches where you can keep track of everything around you." Rupert spoke in a solemn voice to press this point. "Even in the darkest night, your remarkable eyes will let you see as clearly as day! And, Thea, you have a unique ability to turn your head to see behind you!" Rose and Rupert, though neither one of them could demonstrate this remarkable ability, gave the little owl exercises to strengthen her neck muscles. "You'll be able to turn your head to see in any direction without changing the position of your body—very handy. You'll see!"

With the crows' help, Thea was becoming more and more owl every day.

* * * * *

Finally, her feathers were ready for flight lessons. At last, Thea thought. She'd enough of walking everywhere—it was tiring, and it took so long!

"Watch me closely, Thea! Watch what I do with my wings and legs!" And with that, Rose took a few steps and lifted—it seemed like magic—into the air. "Watch again!" Rose repeated the take-off exactly as before. "Now you try, Thea. Don't try to fly far. Just aim for lifting off the ground. That's the first step."

"But how do I land, Rose? I don't want to just flop on the ground! I might hurt myself!"

"Just hold your wings out but stop flapping them. You'll glide to a landing."

Thea hesitated.

"You can do it!" Rose encouraged. "You can do it! Just get started and give it a try."

Thea flailed her wings and legs and, much to her amazement, managed to lift a few inches off the ground.

"Great! Fabulous! You did it!" Rose gave Thea a big hug, and Rupert cheered from the sidelines. "Ready to try again?"

Thea kept trying, and soon she was flying short distances and landing solidly back on the ground. It seemed to come naturally, as long as she took it step by step. And Rose was so very good at breaking the process down into "baby steps."

"Just aim for lifting off the ground."

In a few days, Thea was flying confidently. She could land on the ground or in a tree or on ledges in the tower. *I can fly! I was born to fly! It's soooo fun!*

* * * * *

As far as Colwyn, Itsy, Evie, Emma, and the squirrel girls knew, Thea was still learning owl heritage and basic skills, and Rupert and Rose, at Thea's request, were careful not to contradict that view. Then one day, the crows delivered invitations to the Inn at Ivy Knoll, Rosebud Cottage, and Colwyn's tree trunk hollow for a little celebration at the tower to honor Thea's progress so far.

"What a great idea," responded Emma.

"Wouldn't miss it!" Colwyn beamed. And Itsy smiled widely in agreement.

"How delightful!" Evie voiced her enthusiasm. "I'll bring a cake!"

At the appointed day and time, the group gathered at the base of the tower. Everyone was excited. Lily and Effie couldn't stand still, they were so proud of their little friend. With Rupert standing by, Rose raised a wing for silence, and Thea stepped forward. Evie, Colwyn, Itsy, and the squirrels were expecting a recitation of owl lore. And that's how Thea began. "It may interest you to know..."

Suddenly, with a dramatic flourish, she flapped her wings and gracefully lifted into the air. She silently circled the tower three times, skillfully dipping and soaring, then landed on the very top stone. Absolutely glowing with pride, she raised her wings in triumph. "I can fly! I can fly! I can fly like an owl!"

After a few moments of hushed astonishment, the gathered crowd whistled and cheered. "Hooray! Hooray for Thea! Hooray for our owl!" Everyone raved about Thea's accomplishments—and Rose and Rupert's skill and generosity in serving as her tutors. It was a big day in the community, one that would be remembered and celebrated for years to come.

* * * * *

A few days later, Thea moved to the nest she had built on a ledge inside the tower. Despite Emma's earlier fears about what her girls' reaction to separating from their friend would be, Effie and Lily were simply so proud! For her part, Thea was unspeakably grateful to Emma for taking her in, to Lily and Effie for being such good friends, to her beloved mentors, Rose and Rupert, for teaching her to be an owl, and to everyone in the community for welcoming her and cheering her on. After the tragedy of the storm, this day was the beginning of a new chapter in Thea's life. *I'm so fortunate after all.*

We are not forever bound by the circumstances of our birth. Change is always possible, especially when self-awareness casts a bright light on our lives and points to a new way of being.

In Which Felicia Liberates the Mice

It was a cold, wet, thoroughly miserable day when Cook ventured to the village to do her shopping. She would have liked to postpone her errands, but the kitchen was critically low on several important provisions. There was certainly no guarantee that the weather would improve in the next few days, so she bundled up and, with a scowl showing exactly how she felt about it, ventured out.

Now she was on her way back to the manor house, her shopping finished, her bag full.

The chill aggravated the ache in her hip, and the heavy bag made the pain even worse. The bitter rain stung her face, and she winced. Tears of frustration at her lot in life gathered in her eyes. Then, to make matters worse, a gust of wind stripped the scarf from her neck. By the time she could retrieve it, the scarf was soaked and useless, so she stuffed it in her bag, now even a bit heavier.

Acutely aware of her discomfort, her bitter thoughts turned to the scullery maid back in the warm manor kitchen. *Reason you not out here 'steada me is you be too stupid. A thought in you head be lonely, wunnit? So you's inna warm kitch'n - prob'bly lazin' round, silly cow!* Cook felt resentful, a feeling not foreign to her.

As she turned off the main street of the village, she noticed an odd lump lying in the gutter. Despite her pain, she stooped to take a closer look. It was a cat. A kitten really. She leaned in further. It didn't look too good—wet, dirty, skinny. In fact, it looked sick. Its eyes were crusted, and its breathing was ragged. *You's a mess.* Cook scooped the kitten out of the gutter and thrust it into her bag. This was not, as it might seem, an act of kindness but a seized opportunity, for a number of mice had recently infested her kitchen and, in fact, the entire lower floor of the manor house. *You be useful mebbe!*

* * * * *

Back at the manor house, Cook found a dirty scrap of blanket and, folding it in half, laid it on the kitchen hearth. She roughly plucked her new possession from

The little kitten fell promptly asleep.

her bag and deposited the kitten on the makeshift bed. "S'pose you need a name. Felix'd do well 'nough." Her mouth curved in the hint of a smile as she briefly remembered a cat she had as a young girl, long ago, before life got so hard. But the pleasant memory was soon gone. "Don't get too comf'table. This ain't no fancy schmancy shelter. Don't work hard? Don't do what you's told? Back to the gutter—like that!" Cook snapped her fingers in the kitten's face and stomped off.

She found two small bowls, one cracked and one chipped. *Wouldn't wanna waste good bowls on a cat!* She filled the chipped one with water, and in the cracked one she placed a bit of chicken skin from the previous evening's downstairs supper. She unceremoniously plunked the two bowls near the blanket scrap. The little kitten ate greedily then, lying on what was the most luxurious bed she'd ever slept on, little 'Felix,' despite her painful runny eyes and ragged breathing, fell promptly asleep.

The next morning, the kitten was pleased to find more scraps in her bowl. After a few days of regular food and a warm place to sleep, she was beginning to feel better. She groomed herself. That grooming was the start of her recovery in earnest. Soon, her pretty sea-green eyes were clear and bright, her marmalade coat was shiny and smooth, and she was growing stronger and more active every day. She knew she had been very fortunate, that she could well have died in that miserable cold wet gutter. But here she was - no longer a pitiful waif, but a proper cat with a proper home!

* * * * *

The young cat was grateful and, in return, uncomplainingly did what was asked of her. What was asked of her was simple. "You job be killin' mice. All 'em!" instructed Cook.

"Yeah, an' no goin' easy!" A glint of evil flashed in the scullery maid's eye as she slammed her palm down on the table as though crushing a mouse. "Like 'at, innit?" *Ow!* She rubbed her palm, which was stinging badly.

The cat didn't have any trouble following this simple instruction. She found mice fascinating. For reasons that she didn't understand but also didn't question, she was almost driven to catch them and was actually quite good at it! Whenever Cook or the scullery maid screeched "Mouse!!!" she sprang into action, and before you knew it there was one less mouse at Milkweed Manor.

After a few weeks, a thought—an unfortunate thought from the cat's perspective—occurred to Cook. *Why cat be eatin' kitchen scraps? Got mice fer supper innit?* Cook reasoned cutting back on the table scraps would encourage Felix to catch more mice. But actually, all reasoning aside, the idea greatly appealed to her mean, nasty nature. *No cat livin' no high life 'round here! Don't see me livin' no high life, don't see nob'dy livin' no high life. What's good fer Cook, too good fer cat!*

A *status quo* settled among the kitchen trio, and all was stable for a number of months.

* * * * *

The cat was now a young adult and continued to do her duty. Whether by inclination, hunger, or a combination of the two, she kept the kitchen and pantry—in fact, the whole of the downstairs—free of mice. It worked well enough. She was grateful for a warm place to sleep. Though understandably disappointed that the supply of table scraps was now nearly nonexistent, she was nonetheless appreciative of whatever came her way, for she was, by nature, a loving and grateful creature.

Then one morning a typical occurrence wakened something in the young feline.

Cook was screaming at the scullery maid. "What be wrong w' you? Never do nothin' right! I say dice, d-i-c-e, the taters! Taters ain't diced, no way!" There was a loud jarring crash as Cook threw the pan of potatoes onto the floor.

The indignant scullery maid was crying but managed to do a little screeching of her own. "You be meanest pers'n what me ever see." She flailed her clenched fists and stamped her foot. "Make me mis'rble, you be happy! You..." she cast about for the proper word, not so insulting that Cook would fire her, but insulting enough to get her point across, "a witch! A mean ol' uglee witch!"

Cook took a threatening step closer. The scullery maid cringed, *mebe went too far!* "Settle youself an' clean up this mess. Then d-i-c-e them taters. Gots you 'nuff wits fer that, stupid cow?" Ensuring she had the final word, Cook turned and stomped out of the room.

"Whacha lookin' at, cat?" The scullery maid, venting her anger and frustration on the creature next lower in the pecking order, aimed a vicious kick at the cat. She put lots of fire behind that kick, and when it failed to make contact, she lost her balance. She pumped her arms frantically, trying to avoid the inevitable, but failed and fell bum first on the hard floor.

Having avoided injury, the cat knew better than to visibly react, although she did enjoy a silent chuckle and savored a jab at the appalling grammar she was subjected to day after day. *Just desserts, innit?* She made her way to the hearth and pretended to fall asleep. Actually, she was on alert for further trouble—which thankfully didn't materialise.

Her duties done for the time being, she lay on her bed for a little nap but instead found herself replaying the scene over the "diced" potatoes. *Whatever that means.* When she'd first arrived here, these episodes of disharmony startled and frightened her, but she soon found she was able to avoid physical injury and began simply ignoring them. This morning though, for whatever reason, she contemplated the sorry fact that discord was a regular, almost constant part of downstairs life.

On that rainy late winter morning when Cook scooped her out of the gutter and brought her to the manor, she believed Cook had saved her life. She was grateful. She was also hopeful, expecting to become part of a family—the downstairs family.

Displaced when she was still so young, her experience with family was limited, but one thing was clear. Though the family of her youngest days lacked most comforts, there was much love. She knew with absolute certainty her mama loved her, her brothers, and her sisters. She, in turn, loved all of them. There were many desperate times, but love kept them going.

It was equally clear there was no family here. She had come to understand that she was being used, not loved. Not loved? She wasn't even seen! On the rare occasions Cook or, less frequently, the scullery maid deigned to call her by name, they insisted on calling her 'Felix.' Apparently, their prejudice that most ginger tabbies were boys overcame their ability to see what was right in front of them—she was a girl! She was Felicia!

* * * * *

Then there was another incident.

One morning when Felicia was resting on her blanket and the scullery maid, scowling dramatically, was scrubbing pots, a mouse happened to amble across the kitchen floor. The little creature seemed to calculate that by moving slowly he wouldn't be noticed. And it worked for a short distance. But then Felicia noticed him out of the corner of her eye. In a flash, the mouse was no more.

This was not an extraordinary event, but what happened next was extraordinary indeed. The scullery maid began laughing. Felicia was startled. She had never witnessed either Cook or the scullery maid indulge in a single moment of merriment.

"Oh, lookee!" screeched the scullery maid. "Jus' saddest thing innit? Po' mouse! Ha ha ha!"

Felicia didn't see anything funny about death. She carried out her mouse control duties, but always with a solemn attitude and a silent prayer for the deceased.

Then the scullery maid pointed to a dark corner of the room, her hand shaking with gleeful emotion, and laughed so hard her eyes teared up. "Oh, no! Lookee! There be th' fam'ly! Trag'dy, innit! Po' family! Ha ha ha!" She scrunched her features into a not very convincing sad look, then, grabbing her side, bent over with the pain of laughing so hard.

Felicia turned her attention to the corner to which the scullery maid pointed. Five mice huddled there, one adult and four youngsters. For the first time, she saw more than mouse-shaped objects. She saw living creatures. Looking into their eyes, something she had never done before, she recognised fellow souls. There was emotion in those eyes—pain and fear. She saw a closely bonded family, now suffering from the cruel loss of one of their own. *These mice are living, sentient beings, just like I am. Wow. This changes everything.*

That night as she lay on her bed by the fireplace, Felicia considered her discovery. She knew it was important, potentially even life changing. She understood that hunting for her food was part of her nature. But now, realising that she was ending the lives of fellow beings, she viewed her kitchen duty as distasteful at the least. As she continued to ponder her actions, she was beginning to feel they were wrong. But how could doing what came naturally be wrong? What would she—should she—do? This was an open question, but she sensed that her life was changing.

* * * * *

The next morning as Felicia patrolled the perimeter of the kitchen garden, she saw Roxanne by the low stone wall at the back of the lawn. The cat knew this raccoon. She lived in the community in the nearby woods and was a regular visitor to the manor house's rubbish heap. Scrutinizing the heap's contents was her favorite activity. She was looking for anything that would be a tempting addition to her stock in the mercantile she ran back in the community. She viewed collecting as her passion, her calling, actually. On this bright beautiful morning, she was absorbed in her search.

As Felicia approached her friend, she could see from the bulges in Roxanne's bag she had already found several promising pieces.

For both friends, their chance meetings were pleasurable indeed. The raccoon enjoyed conversations almost as much as she enjoyed the rubbish heap and had often entertained Felicia with stories of goings-on in the community. To Felicia, it sounded like a wonderful place, a peaceful place full of love and acceptance. Consumed, however, by her duties, she had never found time to visit.

"Felicia, look what I've just found." Felicia stepped closer as Roxanne handed the treasure to her.

The cat inspected the item, handling it very carefully, as it was clearly quite valuable to her friend.

"What is it, Roxanne?"

"It's a watch fob—a piece of a device humans use to tell time! They're often intricately embellished and really quite beautiful." Roxanne's eyes sparkled with excitement. With difficulty, she moved her gaze from her treasure to Felicia's face, expecting to see her own excitement mirrored there. And, indeed, Felicia's eyes sparkled too. But Roxanne immediately recognized the sparkle of tears.

"Oh, Felicia! What is it? What's wrong?"

"Those poor mice," Felicia sobbed. She felt close to breaking with sorrow and guilt. "They haven't done anything wrong! They're just trying to keep tiny body and tiny soul together, as we all are. They love their families and want to keep them safe. Yet that miserable excuse for a human being, Cook, and the equally lacking scullery maid, go after them with a vengeance. And, worst of all, I am the appointed executioner."

"I'm so sorry to hear this. You're such a kind and loving soul I can't even imagine how hard this has been on you, my poor dear." Roxanne drew Felicia close to comfort her.

Through her broken sobs, Felicia continued. "In the beginning, when Cook brought me to the manor, I thought she had saved me. I did what was required of me to get along and to have a home and a family all my own. But what a dysfunctional 'home' it is, and I'd never call it a 'family!' I just can't do it anymore, Roxanne! Somehow, somehow I must save them." She slumped on the ground and covered her face with her paws. Then she added in a defeated voice, "But I don't know how!"

Roxanne, being both clever and practical, was silently thoughtful for a moment. As she took another quiet moment, she switched from collector to problem-solver. "You need to permanently move them out of harm's way." She raised her paw, anticipating what Felicia's response would be. "I know you're going to ask how, but for now all I'm prepared to say is meet me here in three day's time—same time, same place. And in the meantime, no killing! Try to just scare them into hiding."

Felicia would do the best she could.

* * * * *

When they met a few days later, Felicia was bursting with curiosity about Roxanne's plan. With a sly smile lighting her face, the raccoon handed her a little bundle carefully wrapped in white paper and tied with a red and white candy cane string.

Felicia unwrapped it but was at a loss for something intelligent to say! "What is it?" she finally blurted out as she curiously examined the item, turning it round and round in her paws.

"Pockets," Roxanne replied, and for emphasis, pretending to stuff both her front paws in the pockets of a pretend apron. "One of the most important developments in all of history! Pockets are definitely needed in this situation!"

Felicia realised it must be some sort of garment. There were loops—possibly for her front legs—and straps—possibly to fasten under her belly. But the odd thing was that the part which would lay over her back was covered with little pockets! This much she could see, but still it was a mystery!

"Listen carefully, Felicia. We both know that many lives depend on the success of this plan. On the night of the next full moon, put this pack on. Be sure the loops are secure around your legs and the straps are tight around your belly. It's a sort of saddle for the mice! A saddle for their escape. It's how you'll bring them to the community.

"Have the mice climb up and settle into the pockets. Appoint one of the more responsible mice to watch over the others to ensure that everyone stays put in their pockets. It will be an exciting adventure for them, but for success, it's crucial that they all remain quiet and still. Any roughhousing could put you off balance and cause a fall. Any noise could alert Cook or, even worse, the groundskeeper with his shotgun. Be sure everyone is secure in the pockets and understands the ground rules before you begin to move!

"When everyone is loaded up and settled down, head to the rubbish heap. Walk slowly, and as smoothly as you can. When you get to the heap, you'll see an arrow pointing into the forest. There will be many more laying out a path for you.

The raccoon handed her a carefully wrapped bundle.

Follow the path to its end, and there a group of animals will be waiting to welcome the mice to their new home!"

"That's the plan. I'll take care of preparations in the community. Everything will be ready to receive them. That's the easy part, though! How you convince the mice to go with you is the hard part—and your problem!"

And Felicia knew it would be a big one. She had harmed, actually killed, mice in the very recent past. How could she convince them to trust her now? Felicia knew it would take time, careful planning, and small steps to gain the mice's trust. Fortunately, there were many days until the next full moon.

* * * * *

Over the next few days, she had several ideas, but as she mentally tested them, she found that each one fell short. Finally, she decided on the obvious approach. She would win them over with food. She stole tidbits from the kitchen until she had a nice little stockpile, then offered the treats to the mice. They, of course, saw it as a trick! She tried tastier and tastier treats to no avail. To the mice, no tasty treat was worth losing their lives!

Finally, with time growing shorter, Felicia decided on a direct appeal. Every time she saw a mouse she would lie very still and speak softly. "Little mouse, I was a danger to you in the past. But I am a danger no more. You have a right to live in safety, and this is not a safe place. There is a loving community not far from here, filled with many different kinds of animals who live together in peace. They offer you a new, safe and happy home, and it would be my honor to take you there.

"Meet me in the shrubbery outside the kitchen door at midnight on the night of the next full moon. Stay in the shadows and be very quiet. I will arrive just a moment after midnight and we'll set off to begin your new life!"

At first the mice ignored her. Then they listened, just barely. Many scoffed at her—*Why should we believe you? Why would you help us?*

But slowly, ever so slowly, James, one of the mouse elders, came around to Felicia's plan. "Life here is precarious indeed. Everyone is against us. We have lost so many friends and family members. Perhaps we should take this chance." With the most respected mouse elders on board, acceptance of Felicia's plan gathered momentum. One by one, the number of mice willing to go to a new home in the forest grew.

* * * * *

The day of the full moon Felicia was nervous—nervous as a cat in a room full of rocking chairs! She smiled at her joke. But the levity was brief. *What if no mice come? What if Cook discovers our plot and comes after us? What if one or more of them gets injured! I can just see her charging towards us, menacingly brandishing a cast-iron pan in each hand, determined to kill! Or the groundskeeper...*

* * * * *

It had been a very long day, but finally it was nearly midnight. Felicia was suited up in her 'Coat of Freedom,' as she had come to call it. She hid behind a tree trunk several feet from the kitchen door and waited quietly for the mice to arrive.

She breathed a sigh of relief when she saw the first mouse move silently into the shrubbery. Then there was another, and another, and before she knew it a mouse crowd was huddled together. Excitement certainly must have been running high in the shrubbery outside the kitchen door, but no on made even the smallest squeak. Old and young, singles and families, adventurers all, they were ready to take their chances and risk the dangers of this night for a new life.

Felicia followed Roxanne's instructions to the letter. The diminutive passengers climbed into the pockets of her Coat of Freedom. James, their leader, and Safety Officer for the relocation venture, had previously met with each mouse who was to join the exodus. He'd explained the ground rules and how important strict adherence would be—perhaps even a matter of life and death. Tonight, once all the mice were on board, James quietly and solemnly ran through those rules again. Everyone was quiet. Everyone was ready.

James climbed aboard. Off they went!

The journey through the night forest was full of exciting things, some beautiful and others scary, but all memorable. The mice marveled at the beauty of the moon shining through the branches of the oaks and beeches, casting shadows and pale light on the forest floor. The sky was breathtaking, full of sparkling stars and splashed with the glory of the Milky Way. But the night was not all beautiful and splendid. At one point they passed the remains of an ancient tree which had long ago been struck by lightning. Only two gnarled branches remained, and in the dim light, that tree morphed into a huge monster reaching its craggy arms menacingly toward the passing party. The mice squealed with alarm as they passed. Then, on top of that, the loud hoot of an owl sent them diving deep into their pockets—except for James, of course, who remained acutely aware of his responsibilities.

The journey through the night forest was full of exciting sights.

By the time Felicia neared her destination, most of the mice had fallen asleep. Soon joyful cries of welcome awakened them. They wearily climbed down out of their pockets. At that very moment, a trio of shooting stars lit the sky over an amazing sight! There, in front of them, they saw a most impressive little building, sturdy and strong, built of stones mortared with mud and clumps of moss. A colorful banner fluttered above the door: "Welcome, Mice!" Inside, the floor was covered with tiny soft blankets, and in the center was a tempting pile of dried corn kernels.

Three of the community members were absent from the festivities that night. Thea, Rupert, and Rose stayed away, as they didn't want to scare the mice. Soon they would all be fast friends. But for tonight they thought their absence would be best. In any case, a large and enthusiastic crowd of smiling forest creatures gathered to celebrate the mice's arrival. There were badgers, squirrels, hares, a raccoon, even a family of mice, and a most impressive rat. Many had signs with messages of welcome, and each voiced a joyous greeting for the new arrivals. "We're so glad you're here!"

"You'll be safe here!"

"Welcome to our community."

"What is this place called?" James asked.

Colwyn reflected, *this impressive, responsible mouse may well become a community leader*, then replied. "This is the animal community in the woods behind Milkweed Manor, and we call it, simply, 'the community,' or sometimes 'Milkweed.' We hope this lodge we built for you will become the center of a little mouse village.

"You must all be exhausted, with the excitement and the late hour. Get a good night's sleep, everyone. We'll be back with you in the morning and begin the happy work of getting you settled."

* * * * *

The next morning, Colwyn and Itsy accompanied the resident mouse family, Thomas, Meg, and their children to the lodge. They arrived just as the mice were finishing their breakfasts of corn kernels. Excited greetings were exchanged all around.

Colwyn made the introductions, then addressed the new arrivals. "Thomas, Meg, and I would like to take you on a short walk to show you where we live." And so, the trio led the way to the twig and leaf nest in a nearby hedge.

"Not long ago," Thomas began, "our previous home was destroyed by a terrifying storm. With the community's help, we built our new home here. The badgers suggested an underground burrow for safety, and we settled on this hybrid design—a leaf and twig nest in the undergrowth built over a 'storm cellar' burrow. Meg would love to give you a tour!"

A steady stream of "oohs" and "aahs" rang out as Meg proudly pointed out the features of her home. Some of the guests focused on the marvels of construction, while others were enchanted with Meg's obvious talent for decorating and keeping a comfortable and welcoming home. The newly arrived mice, being house mice, understood how to build homes within a human structure, but living in the forest was new to them.

Once all the mice had finished touring Thomas and Meg's home, Thomas made a suggestion. "If all of you are in favor, we can help you build your new forest homes in this hedge. We would have a splendid little town of mice. Perhaps we could call it 'Littleton.' Or, since it's in a hedge 'Littleton Hedge.'"

Everyone chattered excitedly and quickly made the decision to do just that! The work began immediately and continued over several days. Each of the community's residents helped, in one way or another, to bring Littleton Hedge into being.

* * * * *

Once Littleton Hedge was complete and all the mice were settled in their new homes, they held a ceremony at the lodge where the community had welcomed them on their first night in the forest. They all enjoyed the delicious cake that Evie made, on which she had written, in her signature pink frosting, 'WELCOME.' The badger boys, Arthur and Percival, stepped forward to proudly present the mice with a surprise.

"This is for you, mice! We made it! It's a sign for over the door of your lodge." It read, 'Littleton Hedge Community Center.' With obvious pride, the badgers hung the sign on the hooks they had installed, unobserved, the day before. The gathered throng cheered—or squeaked, as the case might be—at the fine show of community spirit.

Everyone was thrilled, but Felicia most of all. With her act of compassion and bravery she had become, with her dear friend Roxanne's help, the cat she wanted to be.

* * * * *

After that night, from time to time, new mice inevitably tried to settle in the manor kitchen. Each time, Felicia relocated them to Littleton Hedge. Cook and the scullery maid had no idea about these rescues, and since a mouse in the kitchen was now a rare sight, they paid less and less attention to her—which was fine with Felicia! With her mouse control duties greatly lightened, Felicia was able to spend more and more time visiting her friends, new and old alike, in the community.

'Nobody's perfect' is a truth, but no excuse for bad behavior. 'Boys will be boys' is a trivialization of recklessness. Boys will indeed be boys until responsible adults step in and teach them to be men.

In Which the Badger Boys Behave Badly

It was a joyful day. Even the sky was celebrating with a gentle warm breeze languidly pushing a field of cheerful puffy clouds. There would be a welcome ceremony today. Emma and the squirrel girls prepared by spending the morning baking sweet corn cakes. After lunch, when the little cakes had cooled, the girls lined a basket with a pretty sea-green gingham cloth. They filled the cloth nest with the cakes, then folded the cloth over them. Emma laid a sprig of wildflowers on the top—so pretty! Mid-afternoon, they were ready to set off to Littleton Hedge to help welcome the most recent group of mice that Felicia was saving from the manor kitchen. "Let's go, girls!" Emma called.

All through the community, similar preparations were well under way. Everyone was going! Everyone with the possible exception of the badger twins Arthur and Percival.

Underground at Sweetbrier Sett, a verbal altercation was about to erupt. Aunt Audrey had carefully arranged an impressive array of root vegetable canapes on a lovely etched glass platter, a find from Roxanne's Mercantile. She and her daughter Gwen were nicely dressed and coiffed—in a word, ready to go. Audrey called the boys but when they appeared was appalled to see that they had not yet changed their clothes!

"You're not ready!" Audrey gasped. "We're going to be late! Get ready right now, and quickly."

"But we don't want to go!" whined Arthur.

"It's boring!" glowered Percival.

Aunt Audrey was horrified. "Since when is participating in joyful community events 'boring?' she challenged them.

"Only since about the umpteenth one of these particular shindigs," Arthur responded sarcastically. His tone set Audrey's teeth on edge.

"We'll deal with the consequences later."

But before she could respond, Percival chimed in, "Mice, mice, mice! Who cares?"

And at that, little Gwen who was observing the ghastly scene with saucer eyes, visibly winced. *How can they be so rude to my mum? To my mum who took such good care of them after they were orphaned, and how can they disrespect the community that's so generously welcomed us all?*

Arthur continued defiantly, "We've fulfilled our civic duty long ago. Anyway, Percy and I've agreed that it's a waste of time and," both boys stood up taller and finished in unison, "we're not going!"

Gwen was so shocked that her hair stood on end, threatening to unseat her hair bow. Audrey, however, turned steely. "I don't have time to argue with you. Gwen and I will not be rude to the community by arriving late to the celebration. Do as you please. We'll deal with the consequences later." With that, Audrey picked up the tray of canapes with one paw and took Gwen's paw with the other. They turned and marched proudly towards Littleton Hedge, determined to enjoy a pleasant afternoon despite the bad behavior of others.

* * * * *

Arthur and Percival were surprised at their victory. They exchanged grins of triumph and tore off in the opposite direction, running at breakneck speed, ignoring all rules of the road, not to mention common sense. They were giddy with thoughts of adventure and fun!

The boys sped past the squirrel family who were on their way to the celebration. Lily, the younger of the girls, exclaimed how ill-behaved the badgers were. "Surely those boys are up to no good!" Mama Emma and sister Effie nodded in agreement as the boys disappeared down the path.

It didn't take long for little Lily's prediction to come true!

As the badger boys careened through the garden at the squirrels' beloved Rosebud Cottage, Percival knocked over a plant in a small but beautiful pot. Perhaps it was an accident, or perhaps not. After all, are outcomes from careless behavior really 'accidents' or are they inevitable consequences? In any case, the pot skidded across the path. Then Arthur, who was stumbling after Percival, tripped over it. That additional bit of momentum sent the pot flying. It hit a large rock at the side of the path and smashed into a million pieces, mutilating the plant that Emma had so carefully tended.

The boys, having not yet achieved the character of their names' sakes, broke into fits of laughter. They twirled round, sharing high-fives and pumping their arms in victory. Yes, victory over a potted plant! As they circled, they noticed a whole group of plants—large, medium, and small—each carefully planted in its own beautiful, unique, hand-made pot. Simultaneous flashes of inspiration elicited excited cries from both the boys. "Let's smash them all!"

The fun didn't last long. It took mere moments to destroy what Emma and her girls had nurtured over the years. Nothing remained unscathed. The boys had broken every beautiful pot and mutilated every plant, plants that had been thriving until the arrival of the badger twins.

"Well done, Art!"

"Likewise, Percy!"

Their eyes sparkling with excitement, the bad badgers went on their way, looking for the next opportunity to wreak havoc.

Flying far above, the crows witnessed the whole sorry episode and couldn't help but wonder who would be the next to suffer. As it turned out, the boys were exhausted from their escapades and soon fell asleep in the shade on the edge of a small meadow. They looked so innocent slumbering peacefully among the wildflowers. How deceiving looks can be!

* * * * *

Meanwhile, the mouse welcoming ceremony was proceeding. All the community animals—with the notable exception of two young badgers as well as the crows and Thea the owl—attended, and all were having a fine time, conversing, playing games, and enjoying delicious snacks. The newly arriving mice were all smiles, not only grateful for their deliverance from the mouse-hating cook and scullery maid, but also looking forward to the promise of a secure new life in a loving community.

The ceremony had been so successful that the sun was already setting when Emma and her girls headed home. When they got to their cottage though, there was still enough light to take in the extent of the shocking damage the badger boys had left in their wake.

"Mama! Oh, no! Look what's happened!" shrieked Effie.

"The plants are ruined! Oh, no!" echoed Lily, and they both began to cry. They were shocked at what they saw, but also frightened. "Who could have done this, Mama?"

"Do you think the perpetrators are still around? Do you think they want to hurt us too?" Both girls hid in the folds of Emma's skirt, sobbing and shaking violently.

"Don't worry, darlings. Whoever did this is very bad, but I can't imagine them sticking around to be discovered. I think they're far away by now. They may be brave opponents of helpless plants, but I'll wager they're just cowards at heart." Emma hugged her girls close.

As she comforted her girls, she scanned the scene before her. It took all her strength to not break down in tears herself. Instead, she focused on containing her emotions so as not to further upset her girls.

Despite her brave face, Emma was crushed to realise what had been lost. As her sad eyes took in the devastation, she could barely contain the sobs rising in her throat. Those pots held the secret ingredient for her famed fiddlehead fern and mushroom pie. Cuttings of that herb, along with the recipe for the succulent dish, had been handed down in her family for ages. The pie had been the centerpiece of every holiday celebration for as long as anyone could remember. And, most recently, the pie had warmed the tummy and heart of little Thea soon after her girls found the young owl lost in the woods.

The destruction of that herb meant the end of an era, and it felt like the deepest betrayal of those who had gone before. Anger swelled alongside her sorrow. *How could anyone be so thoughtless, even cruel? How can I ever replace the herbs? Is it even possible? What can I, should I, do?*

As distressed as all the squirrels were, it was, nonetheless, time for the nightly bedtime ritual, and Emma was determined to conduct it as she did every other night. "Let's go inside, girls. It's time for bed. I know you're both tired after such a busy day. And don't worry. Things will seem brighter in the morning."

As was their custom, each girl selected which pajamas she would wear that night. Emma helped Effie into the pair with the purple dinosaurs and Lily into her favorite fairy set. Then she tucked them into their soft beds. They said their prayers together, asking God's blessing on everyone in the community.

"Mama," Lily asked, "do we want God to bless whoever ruined our garden?"

"Yes, dear," Emma replied. "God's blessing is especially important for those who have gone astray."

Each girl selected the pajamas she would wear that night.

Emma pulled the curtains back so the girls could see the moon and stars as they fell asleep. "Good night, girls, and God bless. Don't worry about anything. Nighttime is for peaceful sleep and pleasant dreams." And with that, she kissed each of her precious children goodnight.

With the girls safely tucked in, Emma changed into her softest, coziest nightgown and settled by the fire. She roasted a few pine nuts—comfort food—and allowed herself to finally feel the sadness of recent events, giving full expression to her sorrow. Then she was off to bed. Perhaps her beloved great-grandmama, that enterprising squirrel who had assembled the collection of family recipes, would visit her in a dream and offer guidance. Tomorrow, renewed by a night's rest, she would face the problem head on. She would find a solution.

* * * * *

Early the next morning, Emma and the girls tackled the clean-up. While they were working, Gwen came by to play. Effie and Lily filled their little badger friend in on the disturbing events of the previous day. Emma shared her concern about the loss of the irreplaceable herbs and what they meant to her family. Although the badger boys, Arthur and Percival, were sometimes immature and irresponsible, Gwen was very different. She was a thinker and a doer—some said she was destined for a distinguished career in the law. Or perhaps, with a little polish, a politician!

She immediately pitched in to help with the clean-up, asking probing questions all the while. "When did this happen?"

"Yesterday, while we were at the welcoming in Littleton," Emma answered.

"Then anyone at the welcoming is innocent of this shameful act of vandalism. Who wasn't there?" Gwen, suddenly remembering her brothers had skipped the festivities, quickly deflected. "Could there have been any witnesses?"

The only community members the squirrels could think of who hadn't attended the ceremony were Thea and the crows. And they knew why. Just as at every past such welcoming, the birds didn't want to frighten the newly arrived mice.

Clearly, the perpetrator or—as Gwen sadly added in her own thoughts—perpetrators needed to be found. This kind of behavior was simply not acceptable in their peaceful community. Even though Emma seemed convinced the herbs were irreplaceable, Gwen had another thought on the subject. "Emma, don't give up on replacing the herbs—it's too early for that."

With the clean-up finished, Gwen took Effie and Lily by the paw. "Come with me! I have an idea!"

* * * * *

First stop—Sweetbrier Sett, Gwen's own home. Aunt Audrey confirmed for Effie and Lily what Gwen already knew: that neither Percival not Arthur had attended the welcoming, preferring to go off on their own. She also remembered, under Gwen's skillful questioning, that Percival had returned home with a cut on his left leg. It was so nasty that she applied her special poultice.

It wasn't looking good for Arthur and Percival!

* * * * *

Meanwhile, Emma sat outdoors with a calming cup of tea, thinking sad thoughts about the loss of the herbs. But her reverie was soon interrupted by the crows, Rupert and Rose, who flew down from a large oak tree and alighted next to her. They commiserated about Emma's troubles for a while, then shared that they had seen the brutal event. It had been the badger boys, Arthur and Percival. It started out as an accident—one which any sensible creature could have predicted given the badger boy's out-of-control roughhousing. But then it turned into sheer vandalism. And, wouldn't you know it, one of the boys got a nasty cut on his leg as a reward for all his troubles! The crows were apologetic about not being able to stop the vandalism. They had been flying quite high, and the whole incident happened so quickly!

After tea, Emma gathered her thoughts and set off to the sett to speak with her friend Audrey. Had she been in her usual frame of mind, she would have taken the opportunity of her walk to appreciate the natural beauty all around her. As it was, she was so focused on the coming encounter with her friend she missed the chattering of a trio of fledgling wrens begging a meal from their parents. She missed the heady fragrance wafting from a clump of wild sweet peas growing by the path. And she missed the sight of two young rabbits playing in the grass. Having missed all these delights, she nonetheless arrived at Sweetbrier Sett.

"Welcome, Emma!" Audrey had seen her approaching.

"Thanks, but I come on a sad mission, as I must speak with you about Arthur and Percival."

Audrey already knew most of the story, having been brought up to date by little Gwen, but once Emma added the detail of the cut leg, any lingering doubts were laid to rest. Yes, clearly Arthur and Percival had misbehaved, and misbehaved badly.

An accident was one thing, but purposeful wanton vandalism was quite another. It was time for quick decisive action!

Audrey summoned the boys.

After she presented the evidence and pronounced guilt, she invited Emma to describe the crime and how much the damage had hurt her. Once everyone heard the victim statement, Audrey imposed the sentence—justice was swift but always fair in the community! "You boys will make restitution!"

Yes, that's fair, thought Emma. *But how can they ever replace those herbs?*

The boys had no idea what "restitution" meant, and once Aunt Audrey explained it to them, they were dismayed! How could they fix the pots? They were reduced to smithereens! And how to replace the herbs when they didn't even know what they were? "Well," Aunt Audrey exclaimed, "that's your problem, isn't it? And a problem of your own making, so don't go feeling sorry for yourselves! You'd better put on your most powerful thinking caps and get on with it! Restitution is to be made within the week!"

* * * * *

The community, when it first heard of the vandalism, passed harsh judgment on the unknown perpetrators. But once the animals heard the story and its resolution, their hearts softened—a bit. The badger boys were rowdy, loud, careless, and often oblivious of the results of their actions. But they could also be loving and considerate. Behind the sometimes rough ways of the youths, there was definitely potential. So, assistance started coming to the badger boys from some surprising sources.

Notably, Emma, who was most hurt and had the right to be most angry of all, offered the boys some advice on the pots. She knew they couldn't replace them, but she gave guidance on an alternative solution—building a 'raised bed,' whatever that was!

"Thanks, Emma," Arthur said in quite a subdued voice, "but as for the herbs, we don't know where to look, much less what we're looking for."

"Wait here a moment, boys." Emma disappeared into the cottage and quickly returned with a pencil and small note pad. She drew them a sketch of the herbs, tore it from the pad, and handed it to the boys.

"I don't know how this will help," Emma cautioned. "I've heard these herbs are extinct from the forest around here."

But the boys had an idea.

When the badger twins presented their plan to Thea, Rupert, and Rose, the birds were ready to pitch in, more for Emma's sake than for the badgers'. Armed with Emma's sketch, they flew reconnaissance, determined to locate the herbs. If they existed anywhere within their range of flight, they'd find them!

The three, being exceptionally clever birds, devised a plan for a methodical aerial search that would cover the entire area. And, with Colwyn organizing the effort on the ground, the inhabitants of Littleton Hedge pitched in by setting up refreshment and relaxation stations placed strategically along the birds' flight path. Throughout the day, Colwyn made his way from station to station bringing fresh supplies and checking that all was progressing smoothly.

Day one passed with no finds. Day two passed with no results, and the birds were tired and discouraged. They set off on the third morning without much expectation. The day wore on. They rested at the refreshment stations for lunch, then started their afternoon with heavy hearts.

Not long into the afternoon's search though, Rupert's triumphant caw perked everyone up. It heralded a find. The mice at the nearest station scampered off to fetch Emma and when she arrived, she found all three birds standing in a circle around a clump of beautiful soft green herbs. The leaves were quite distinctive, with a leaf shaped somewhere between a heart and an arrow. "That's it!" Emma exclaimed excitedly, twirling in a circle, her tail spreading gloriously around her.

Aunt Audrey, hearing of the find, dispatched Arthur and Percival to the discovery site to retrieve some of the plants. She gave them strict instructions to remove just a few, to pack them carefully in damp cloths for the journey, and, especially, to be sure they left the remaining plants in good condition with any holes around them filled in completely. The boys seemed to be listening intently. 'Restitution' was making a big impact on both of them.

Acquiring the herbs was a huge step forward, but it was only part of what was required of them. They also needed something in which to plant them.

* * * * *

A little while later, walking back, they saw two large rocks in the shade of a beech tree. Tired after retrieving the plants and carefully following all associated instructions, they sat down for a bit. It was a beautiful afternoon with the shade dappling the ground. Sweet-voiced birds sang in the trees, and a light breeze ruffled thick clumps of bright green grasses. Bees buzzed in the warm air. The boys might

To say the least, Arthur was feeling dejected.

have enjoyed all this beauty surrounding them had they noticed it. But their spirits were flagging. It seemed there had been nothing but work, work, work for as long as they could remember, and not a spot of fun to relieve the monotony.

To say the least, Arthur was feeling discouraged. "Well, it's nice to have the plants of course, but what in the world will we plant them in since we smashed all the pots? I don't see how we'll ever get this done. And we desperately need to get it done soon because ever since our little mistake all we've been doing is working with no time at all to play!"

"I know," commiserated Percival. "It's been a bad couple of days. But to tell you the truth, the worst parts were the devastation in Emma's eyes and the disappointment in Aunt Audrey's. Once this is all behind us, and as much as I hate to suggest it, maybe we'd better think about how to mend our ways!"

Arthur scowled. *Percy! That doesn't sound like fun at all!*

Their depressed discussion continued as they considered what to plant the herbs in. Then Arthur, vaguely recollecting Emma's suggestion about a 'raised bed,' had a flash of what he thought might be genius. "See that wall over there, Percy? What if we took some of the stones and arranged them in a circle? Then we could fill the circle with dirt and plant the herbs inside it."

"Brilliant!" exclaimed Percival. In his mind's eye he could almost see light at the end of the dreary work tunnel. "But think about taking that idea a little further. What if we stack a second circle on top of the first? That'd raise the plants higher off ground level and they'd seem bigger. Maybe that would earn us more points!"

* * * * *

Rested and armed with a plan for how to proceed, they delivered the herbs to Rosebud Cottage. It would have been so nice to stop for the day and continue first thing in the morning, but Emma said, "No. The plants need to get back in the ground as soon as possible or they'll dry out and die."

Disappointed, the boys headed back into the forest for the mossy rocks. They had to make so many trips! And the rocks were blasted heavy! But at last they had gathered enough for their project. It turned out they needed a few more so had to make one final trip, but in the end, the little two-story circle was ready.

Being badgers, they were experts at digging and soon excavated enough rich dirt from a nearby bank to fill the circle. Just as dusk was falling, Emma planted the herbs. Miraculously, a soft rain began to fall, and she tipped her face to the sky in gratitude. *Perfect!*

"This gentle rain is the perfect way to water the plants. It's a very good sign for their future health. Boys, your duty is done. You have made restitution in full."

At last! The boys were relieved.

"And, in fact," Emma continued, "the raised bed you built is beautiful—better than pots. It's not breakable!" She wanted to make a point. "So, off with you! Tell your aunt you've finished your task with distinction!"

Despite the rain, Emma sat on the edge of the bed for a while, admiring the plants and giving thanks. The rain was matting her fur and she'd need to spend extra time later brushing it out. But she didn't care. The precious herbs lived once again in a place of honor in Emma's cottage garden.

* * * * *

When the boys dragged their weary selves back to the sett that evening, they barely had the strength to tell Aunt Audrey they had finished their project before falling onto their mattresses of dried grass. They were asleep before their heads hit their pillows.

In the morning, Aunt Audrey roused the boys early, and the three of them, along with little Gwen, set off to Rosebud Cottage. Audrey wanted to ensure Emma approved of the work the boys had done. As they came up the path, they heard the distinctive sound of squirrels singing. As they came closer, they saw Effie and Lily skipping in circles around the newly raised bed happily chanting, "The herbs are back, the herbs are back. It's a happy, happy day!"

Emma liked a tidy, organized garden. She was busy staking the plants with nicely trimmed oak branches and embossing labels on strips of copper. Even though she clearly wrote the plants' botanical name on the tags, '*squirrus salvia nemorosa verde*,' no one knew what it meant other than she. But that was fine. It was an ancient family secret, after all!

"Emma, Effie, Lily!" Audrey greeted the squirrels. "Good morning. What a beautiful day and what a lovely rain last night! The boys tell me they've completed their restitution, and we've come by just to be sure that you're satisfied with their work."

The boys hung back nervously. But Gwen quickly and boldly approached to inspect the construction of the raised bed. She observed the work was careful and thorough. Somewhat surprised, but firmly believing in giving credit where credit was due, she pronounced, "Nice work, boys." The boys rolled their eyes, weary of their cousin's attitude. Somehow, she seemed to think it her mission to keep a close watch on how and what they were doing.

"Hi, Audrey." Emma returned the greeting. "Yes, the herbs are back and looking so healthy and beautiful. Last night's fortuitous rain has thoroughly refreshed the plants from the stress of their move. And it's brightened the moss. But more to the point, yes, I am happy to confirm that Arthur and Percival have completed their task."

"Boys," Emma continued with a wide smile, "you've done it! I must admit I had my doubts, but the herbs are even more beautiful than the ones I had before. And that moss! What a vibrant green! This raised bed is surely the centerpiece of my garden! It's such a relief to have my herbs back, to be able to continue the traditions that have always been so important in our family."

She thought for a moment, seeking just the right tone. "Your vandalism hurt me deeply. You've been able to repair the damage." She paused, looking each boy in the eye to ensure she had their full attention. "But remember, it was with the help of others, especially Thea and the crows who actually found the herbs for you. And then there were the mice and Colwyn supporting the birds in their long three-day quest. Be sure to thank them all! And keep in mind that in future your acts of vandalism may not be so easily repaired—if they can be repaired at all. Please give this some thought. But for now, as Shakespeare said, "All's well that ends well.""

"Who's Shakespeare," the boys asked. Aunt Audrey made a mental note to broaden their education.

*Something bad happens. One realises how
much worse the bad thing could have been.
Then the wake-up call registers. The hand of
God was pointing to something that needs one's
attention.*

In Which Illness Lays Littleton Low

Each morning and evening anyone in the community could look skyward and see
Rupert and Rose, the guardian crows, flying far above. Twice each day they flew
their rounds, alert for any threat to the community they were born to protect. As was
their habit, Rupert circled to the west while Rose launched to the east. They scanned
every meadow, every clearing, every stream, and every corner of the forest. Nothing
in any way disturbing or out of place could escape their attention.

The morning was overcast, and a threatening darkness settled on the
southern horizon. A storm was coming in from the Channel, but it was too early to tell
how bad it would be when it reached the community. Noting the possibly threatening
weather, the crows continued their rounds. It wasn't long before Rose alerted. "Caw
caw caw!" Rupert recognized it as a call not of danger but of distress. Something was
very wrong. He quickly flew to the spot where Rose was hovering. The worried look
in her eye concerned him greatly and when he followed her gaze, he immediately
understood her alarm.

Colwyn, carrying little Itsy in his arms, was hurrying along the path that led
to the ancient oak at the heart of the community. He was a clean rat, well known for
his calm and composed demeanor, but what the crows saw this morning was a
disheveled, unkempt, half-dressed mess. His usual gait was calm and measured, but
this morning he was frenzied, stumbling badly and making very little forward progress.

Rose observed to Rupert, "He looks sick! What do you think could be wrong
with him?"

"He's carrying Itsy! Maybe she's sick!"

The crows dove and alit in front of him. Startled, Colwyn skidded to a
stop.

"Colwyn, what's wrong?" Rupert inquired. "I don't think I've ever seen you
in such a state! Is Itsy alright? Are you ill? Where are you hurrying off to?"

It took the rat a few moments to gain his composure. "Oh, I'm so glad to see you! Itsy and I are fine, but it's terrible. Terrible!"

"What's terrible, Colwyn?" Rupert asked, then gently added, "Why don't you start at the beginning?"

"Yes, good idea. Well, first thing this morning Itsy and I were enjoying our usual walk about. I couldn't help but notice the sky and thought there might be bad weather coming, so I decided to swing by Littleton Hedge. Thomas, Meg, and their girls are away visiting their Grandmum you see, and I wanted to check that their doors and windows were secure for a possible storm. But as I approached the hedge, I noticed something unusual—no one was out and about. As you know, the mice children are usually playing from dawn to dusk. They're so fun to watch! I don't know where they get their energy really. The stamina of youth, I guess." He smiled as he recalled the joyful sight, "But I digress."

As he turned his mind back to the morning's events he began to tremble.

"Take a few deep breaths, Colwyn. We're here to help with whatever's wrong!" Rose spoke in a soothing voice, hoping to calm the badly rattled rat.

"Yes, yes. In. Out. In. Out. Better now." Colwyn glanced from crow to crow then continued his story.

"As I was saying, when I got to the hedge there was no one in sight. But I heard strange sounds—pitiful whimpering. I sat Itsy on the grass a short distance from the hedge and told her to wait there for me. As I moved throughout the hedge, I heard that same sound coming from all the houses. I knocked on one door and, when admitted, a horrible sight confronted me. The children were lying in their beds moaning pitifully, their eyes red with tears, and their tiny paws clutching their tummies. The parents were beside themselves trying, with no luck, to comfort the young ones. I went from door to door, and the story was the same at each house. Oh, it's so awful!"

"So, were all the children sick, Colwyn?" Rose probed.

"As far as I could tell, yes, every single one! Except Itsy, of course, who didn't enter the hedge." Tears filled Colwyn's eyes as he recalled what he had seen.

"And what about the parents?"

"They all seemed well enough—though completely distressed about their children of course."

Rose and Rupert were silent for a few moments as they assessed the situation. Then Rose said, "With the illness so widespread, it seems prudent to call on Reynard and ask for his shamanic ministrations."

"Yes, Rose, excellent plan!" Rupert seconded. "But I think we should also alert the community and ask for volunteers. With so many patients, Reynard may well need extra hands."

Just then, Rose saw the badger boys, Arthur and Percival, coming along the path. They were, no doubt, looking forward to a day of carefree fun. "I'm so glad you've happened along, boys," Rose said. "We have an emergency, and we may need your help! According to Colwyn here, all the mice children at Littleton Hedge are quite ill!"

"But what can we do about that?" Arthur pressed, hoping the crows would send him and Percy on their way. But it was not to be.

"We'd better split into two teams then, Rupert," Rose said, ignoring the young badger's protestations. "You and Arthur fetch Reynard while Percival, Colwyn and I gather the volunteers."

Arthur and Percival shifted from foot to foot and looked at the ground. They were obviously uncomfortable with what sounded like a definitely-no-fun-and-possibly-dangerous venture. Apparently assigned to the shaman-fetching team, Arthur was especially nervous. He'd never seen a shaman, but he'd heard they were eccentric at best, and possibly even scary!

"Percival, you accompany Colwyn to the ancient oak. I'll sound the alarm for the volunteers to join you. Wait there for further instructions." Rose gazed from Colwyn to Percival looking for signs of agreement.

"Yes, good plan," Colwyn agreed. "But I need to take a brief detour to drop Itsy with Emma. I'll be quick!"

Although Colwyn was clearly eager to help, Percival was looking decidedly uncertain. So, Rose addressed a few carefully chosen encouraging words to the young badger. "The mice will really appreciate your help!" Percival managed—somehow—not to roll his eyes.

"Rupert," Rose continued, "guide Arthur to Reynard's encampment. Let the shaman know what's happening at Littleton Hedge and that we need his help. Arthur, you may need to show him the way to the hedge and, even though Reynard has his apprentice, they may very well need your help carrying supplies."

Rose had a commanding voice and an expertise in giving orders—as well as a liking for it! She gave Arthur an encouraging squeeze on the shoulder then lifted immediately into the air to begin her task. All the others were quick about their business, appreciating 'time was of the essence.'

* * * * *

Of the badger boys, Percival had the easier task, travelling with Colwyn over familiar paths. Arthur, however, was off into the unknown and none too eager about it. I know Rupert will protect me, but I'd sure feel better if I could fly like he can!

Rupert led Arthur in a direction the young badger had never travelled. Not only had he never been this way, but Aunt Audrey had explicitly warned the boys against it, explaining this part of the forest was thick, dark, and rumored to be dangerous in vague but convincing ways. "Rupert, are you quite sure this is the way? Will we be safe? I've never been this way before!" Poor Arthur's voice broke as he appealed to the crow.

"Yes, of course. I'm familiar with every part of this forest and know exactly where we're going. It's perfectly safe. Don't worry! And pick up the pace! We need to get help for those mice right away!"

Arthur, however, was not reassured. The trees were large and menacing, festooned with garlands of gray moss and large clumps of mistletoe. The shade was deep with very little sunshine permeating the canopy. Though Arthur knew it was morning, it seemed like dusk and, to make matters worse, the forest echoed with strange sounds. A rare few of those sounds were pleasant. Most were eerie at best and a fair share were downright frightening. A call somewhere between a fox's scream and an owl's hoot echoed through the forest. Arthur started shaking.

Arthur wished for the comfort of his twin's presence—they were rarely separated. On the other hand, he thought no, I'm glad you don't have to endure this, Percy!

It was cold in this part of the forest and the young badger's shaking escalated to an unrelenting shivering. A light mist obscured the way. Twisting ribbons of fog rose menacingly from the forest floor, catching at Arthur's feet, frightening him and causing him to stumble. The mist deepened. It was impossible to see more than a few feet in any direction. Left to his own devices, Arthur would have surely turned back long before now. But with Rupert accompanying him, pride didn't leave him any choice other than to continue, placing his hopes in the crow's protection.

Arthur was fervently wishing to be anywhere else when something large began taking shape through the mist. Rupert, uncharacteristically on foot to best guide the young badger, picked his way through the dense undergrowth with Arthur creeping behind. Drawing closer, they began to make out an encampment of the strangest sort. Now a mere few feet away, they saw a building—but a building with walls and roof at odd angles. Parts of it appeared to be stone, other parts, wood, and still other parts simply unidentifiable. A rickety lean-to stood against—or perhaps held up—one of the walls. There were jumbles of strange items everywhere, hanging from the rafters, jammed into baskets, stuck in makeshift pots, drying on racks. Cattywampus shelves held a mismatched array of jars with bizarre contents, each labelled in a script that neither the crow nor the badger could read.

Curiosity began to displace Arthur's fears. What a strange place! This must be where the shaman lives...

* * * * *

Just then a sharp-featured, yellow-toothed creature poked its pointy nose out the closest window giving Arthur—and even Rupert—quite a start. "Whom do you seek and what do you want?" the weasel hissed. "Visitors are rare here, and not always welcome!" Arthur was clearly out of his depth. Rupert stepped forward to address the menace. Arthur stumbled backwards and let out a sigh of relief.

"Vicious, is Reynard about? We're here on a matter of great concern and urgently need his help!"

"Depends on whose calling's my guess! Who are you?" When Vicious was on duty, his desire to protect his master trumped polite discourse.

"As I expect you already know, Vicious, I'm Rupert, one of the guardians of the community behind Milkweed Manor. This is my young companion, Arthur."

"And what, exactly, is it that you want?" Vicious persisted.

At that, a voice boomed from inside the dwelling. "Very good, Vicious. You may stand down. We well know Rupert and I've heard of his young companion. Let's hear them out!"

The door creaked open revealing a fox in a wrinkled and stained tunic, a tunic which may have been white at some point in the past. A bleary-eyed old owl, unceremoniously awakened from his day's sleep by the intrusion, perched precariously on the fox's shoulder. As the owl blinked rapidly, attempting to rise to

"Whom do you seek, and what do you want?"

consciousness, the shaman stared at the visitors with the most piercing pale blue eyes. Arthur nearly fainted.

"Well, what's the big emergency?" Reynard queried. "I haven't got all day! I'm preparing to brew a batch of one of my most popular potions! Time is precious, you know."

"Several mouse families," Rupert began "have recently relocated to our community from the manor house and when our resident rat, Colwyn—you may have heard of him—visited the mice this morning, he found all the young ones confined to their beds. They just lie there, tears streaming down their cheeks, moaning pitifully, sweating from the forehead, and clutching their tummies. The parents are beside themselves!"

Reynard, making a 'come on' motion with his paws, impatiently urged Rupert on.

"Rose and I immediately thought of you and your healing skills. The mice need your help most desperately!"

"Yes, yes, easily dealt with." Reynard closed his eyes and thought for a moment. "We'll need strips of clean cloth, warm water, and honey. Vicious, prepare the digestive distress packs right away! I imagine we'll need as many as a few dozen. And fetch my treatment kit as well. Chop, chop! This strapping young badger can help carry the packs. Always good to have strong young help! Give me a minute to get properly attired."

A few minutes later, Reynard reappeared in the doorway—in full shamanic regalia. A hooded cape reached nearly to his ankles. It seemed quite shabby. The brown fabric was coarse, wrinkled, and dirty with poorly applied patches here and there. But as he took a few steps forward, the cape swung from side to side revealing the lining which, in contrast to the outside of the cloak, was quite sumptuous—the plushest velvet in a sumptuous red-violet colour. Gold embroidered symbols flashed here and there.

The boots were lush black suede. Their red-violet cuffs matched the cloak's lining. A leather cord secured the boots, lacing around a double row of small silver buttons, each decorated with a symbol similar to those embroidered on the cape lining.

The head dress was quite attention-getting. It was constructed around a pair of five-point antlers. Clumps of bright spring-green moss covered their base. A dozen pheasant feathers seemed to grow from the bottom of one of the antlers, forming a wide fan. The top-most feather pointed straight upwards while the lowest one sat at a jaunty angle curving over Reynard's cheek. A large sparkling crystal hung from one of the antler points.

Reynard leaned on an elaborate walking stick which appeared to be made of an ancient oak branch. The maker had stripped it of its bark and lovingly oiled it to reveal the sinuous grain of the wood. The stick had a tip of gleaming silver. An ivory wolf head formed the grip—the eyes were garnets faceted in an antique style. The stunning object was clearly quite old, and dazzled Rupert.

"No need to stare!" Reynard scolded. "But I do cut a striking figure, do I not? Where are we headed?"

Rupert told Reynard that Arthur would lead them, but also gave him directions in case Arthur got confused which was, quite frankly, entirely possible given Arthur's rattled state of mind. With that, Rupert flew off to alert the community to prepare for the shaman's arrival.

"Rupert, wait! Arthur cried. He was terrified to be left alone with this strange pair.

"You'll be fine, Arthur!" Rupert, already airborne, cawed from a distance.

* * * * *

Whilst Rupert and Arthur were fetching the shaman, Rose and Percival gathered volunteers at the ancient oak. The crowd was buzzing with concern. Finally, Rupert appeared with the shaman's instructions. Rose thought the most efficient approach would be to get the required items from the manor house, so she sent Percival to fetch Felicia. "Tell her we need honey and strips of clean cloth. Repeat that back to me, Percival. It's important that you don't forget anything."

Bored by just standing around and ready to at last be part of the action, the badger confidently proclaimed, "Honey and clean cloth. Honey and clean cloth. Honey and clean cloth. Yes, I've got it!"

"Excellent!" Rose was impressed, and surprised. "Take a few helpers with you and get going now! The rest of us will proceed to Littleton Hedge and begin heating water."

When Felicia, Percival, and his helpers arrived at Littleton Hedge, a mouse was busy heating water in a large cauldron. Other mice received the cloth from Felicia and began tearing it into strips. Nothing had been forgotten. All was ready for Reynard.

* * * * *

"I do cut a striking figure, do I not?"

The Shaman's arrival caused quite a stir. The shyer among the crowd nearly swooned at the sight of the pair. They found Vicious, who really couldn't help his menacing appearance, especially frightening. A few of the sick children, roused by the commotion, peered out their windows in astonishment. Who are they? the youngsters wondered.

Reynard got right down to business. Vicious stood at his side ready to do whatever would be required of him, while Arthur, suddenly feeling important, made quite a show of arranging the digestive distress packs within Reynard's easy reach.

The shaman and his assistant were too big to fit into the mouse homes. "Ladies, would you be so kind as to bring a half dozen or so of the patients to me?" Reynard asked, addressing Emma and Evie who were among the volunteers. "I need to question several so I can reach a diagnosis and determine the appropriate treatment." Emma brought the first one and gently laid her on the ground. Then they brought more patients, all from different families, until, as requested, they had assembled about half a dozen.

Reynard approached one of the young mice. She was clearly wary of this strange and strangely outfitted creature. "What's wrong, little one? Where does it hurt?" the shaman asked. His soothing manner soon put her at ease.

"My tummy hurts so bad! And I feel so hot, then I feel so cold. But mostly my tummy hurts badder than it's ever hurt before! Squeak squeak!" Vicious stood beside Reynard taking careful notes, and Arthur stood beside Vicious feeling very important.

"And when did your tummy start hurting?" Reynard continued.

"Just before supper, squeak squeak. I couldn't eat my dinner!" The other patients nodded in agreement.

Reynard continued his examination. "And what did you do yesterday afternoon?"

"It was such a pretty day! We went into the forest. We all played games in a clearing and then collected berries and tiny little apples. We had a picnic. Squeak squeak! It was so much fun!" With only minor variations, it was the same story from each little one.

* * * * *

They assembled more patients until they had about half a dozen.

Now that Reynard had gathered the facts, it was time for hm to develop a diagnosis. He officiously crossed his paws over his chest and closed his eyes. After a brief pause, soft howling sounds rose from his throat followed by a soft yelp. "It's just as I thought! Vicious, get the digestive distress packs."

"They're right here, sir," Arthur excitedly interjected.

"Then, Vicious, bring me hot water and strips of clean cloth." The weasel went scrambling to obey orders and mere moments had passed before the water and cloth strips were ready at the shaman's side.

Reynard burrowed in his treatment kit for his stirring stick then studied the pot of hot water. He judged how many digestive distress packs the water would absorb. "Arthur, empty three of the packs into the cauldron." This is so cool! Arthur swelled with pride and efficiently did as he was bidden. Reynard shredded an aromatic chunk of bark and added it to the pot as well, chanting softly as he worked.

"Cloth strips, please, Vicious!" The weasel carefully dropped several into the hot brew. The shaman stirred them around with his special stick, ensuring that the strips were thoroughly saturated with the healing liquid.

One by one, Emma and Evie carried the sick children to Reynard. Vicious gave each child a spoonful of honey, then Reynard, with more gentleness than one might believe possible, wrapped the child's throat with a warm herb-soaked strip of cloth. He placed his right forepaw on the child's throat and uttered a few unintelligible syllables. A small nod and smile told the child he was finished.

"Go back to bed now, little one," Reynard advised, "and sleep soundly. You'll have pleasant dreams, then will wake in the morning feeling better." Unfailingly, each patient shyly squeaked a subdued thanks, and the parents gratefully carried their child back home for a healing night's sleep.

Very little escaped Reynard who had noticed a sharp contrast between the demeanour of the two badger boys. Arthur, in the thick of things, stood tall and proud, while Percival, occupying the sidelines, shifted restlessly. The shaman summoned the downcast badger. "Percival, I have a task for you, assuming you're available."

"Yes, sir!" Percival straightened and stepped forward eagerly.

"Please visit each mouse house and ask one of the parents to reassemble here. I have some advice for them."

Percival scurried away and soon a large crowd of mouse parents stood before the shaman.

"Mice," Reynard began in a solemn tone. He kept his voice low and spoke slowly to ensure the mice's attention. "I understand you are house mice relocated from the manor house to this forest. That is all very fine. I'm sure you are safer here in many ways. But, as you can see, not in all.

"As house mice, you were born with skills and knowledge to help you survive in a human environment. But life is quite different here. There are both opportunities and dangers that you know nothing about. For example, the 'tiny little apples' your children so enjoyed on their picnic. You see, they are not apples at all, but mildly toxic berries that cause painful tummy distress! There is much to learn to live here safely. Until you can acquire this knowledge, you should limit your activities in the forest. That's my advice, plain and simple—but wise!"

* * * * *

Vicious gathered their belongings and bid farewell to Arthur. "Good job, boy! Hope to see you again!" All the crowd, but especially Colwyn and the mouse parents, graciously thanked Reynard.

Reynard modestly took his leave. "You're most welcome. Vicious and I are at your service, and the crows know where to find me. We're off now. Toodle-oo!" Satisfied with a job well done, they headed into the forest towards their encampment.

The mouse parents were immensely grateful, but also intensely aware they had much to learn to be truly safe in Littleton Hedge. But how would that happen? They were talking solemnly among themselves when Colwyn offered a suggestion.

"Mice, dear friends, don't worry! Remember that Thomas and Meg here, the family that originally welcomed you to Littleton Hedge, are forest mice."

Thomas stepped forward and continued. "Yes, and we are well aware of the 'ins' and 'outs' of life in the meadows and forests. We'll be happy to organize training for both you and your children. We'll teach you what's safe to eat and what's not, where it's safe to go and where it isn't, what to watch and listen for, and how to find your way after dark—and—anything else we or you can think of!"

The assembled mice murmured their agreement.

Thomas continued. "Fortunately, the crows knew Reynard and was able to acquire his assistance. And, as it turned out, this illness was easily cured and apparently has no lasting effects. That was lucky—in more ways than one! It's been a fortuitous wake up call."

He paused, nodded to Meg, then continued. "Meg and I are at your service. If you can select a few of your own to work with us, we'll put the training together right away!"

With that, four of the mouse parents stepped forward. The Forest Safety Training Committee was formed and ready to get to work. In fact, they scheduled their first meeting for the very next day at Thomas and Meg's home. "We'll make this work!" Meg declared, already enthusiastically planning hospitality for the next day.

* * * * *

The night passed quietly and without incident. The next morning was such a contrast from the morning before—there was no peace and quiet to be found at Littleton Hedge! Instead, the happy, exuberant sounds of children playing filled the air.

At Sweetbrier Sett, the badger boys had a lie in after their exciting adventure-filled day. When they woke, the two exchanged stories of their experiences. Both boys embellished their tales, but Arthur had far more material to work with.

Arthur, who had been shaking with fear through much of the previous day, in hindsight viewed the whole experience as a grand adventure. Percival, who at the time was grateful to have not been selected to venture deep into the forest, was a bit jealous. Both, who had at first been dismayed at being drafted into Rupert and Rose's venture, were now grateful to have had a part in the great healing at Littleton Hedge.

Those who are lonely imagine the whole world filled with happy couples. It's an illusion. There are many lonely hearts. The good news is that they can find each other.

In Which an Unlikely Friendship Blooms

Vicious had been sleeping soundly but was now drifting from sleep to wakefulness—that magical time when the day's first impressions take form in one's mind. Happiness overwhelmed him as he realised something. He opened his eyes and saw the first glorious rays of sunlight breaking through the thinning fog and tentatively peeking through his window. He would have appreciated any morning heralding a sunny day, but this one was special. It was his day off!

Stretching and yawning, he rose to a sitting position, then swung his legs over the edge of his ragged cot, feeling for the wool felted slippers that Reynard had given him last Christmas. He traded his striped nightshirt for his cleanest, though not that clean, tunic. Running his paws through his fur, he gave himself a quick grooming, then, softly humming his favorite song, left his lean-to and walked the short forest path to the workroom.

* * * * *

As he expected, his master, Reynard the shaman, was already at work.

There was a constant, pressing workload in the encampment. Preparing an extensive inventory of ingredients for potions was complicated and time-consuming. There were herbs to gather from the forest, then dry and crumble. There were feathers to pickle. There were shed snake skins—Reynard firmly believed in concocting only cruelty-free potions—to scrape the scales from then sort by colour. The pile of beech bark chunks was alarmingly large! Shredding them was hard work, but the most physically demanding task was grinding stones and rare earth to fine powders.

In addition to preparing the ingredients, they also packaged them. Vicious cleaned all the containers. Reynard prepared the labels, as his assistant hadn't yet acquired the skill of writing.

"Ho, Vicious! Have a good sleep? There's a lot on our plate this morning. Our supply of shredded beech bark is alarmingly low."

"Ho, Vicious! Have a good sleep?"

"Well, Reynard, I must remind you that today is my day off! However, if we're facing an emergency I can reschedule and stay here to help."

"No, no, Vicious! You've certainly earned your time off. I just forgot! Off you go." Reynard turned back to the worktable, but then added, "By the way, if you should happen on any morels, could you please collect a few? They'd be scrumptious with our supper."

"Yes, sir!" Vicious affirmed as he headed back to his lean-to to fetch his collection bag.

* * * * *

Days off were rare for Vicious. The never-ending work pressure was one reason. But also, his master needed him. Reynard's shamanic duties kept him on call 24/7, and an emergency could require the shaman's presence at any time. If Vicious were not available to accompany him, it could be extraordinarily demanding for the fox. Reynard was beginning to feel his age.

Despite the backlog of work, Vicious was determined to put it all out of his mind for this one day. As much as he enjoyed Reynard's company, he savoured a bit of time alone and intended to enjoy it with a nice walk around the forest.

Leaving the shaman's encampment, he soon came to nearby Three Frogs' Hollow. Reflecting the place's name, sure enough, there were the three frogs on a log in a small pond. Mist and fog still clung to the damp ground. Nonetheless, the sun was trying valiantly to break through.

"'Morning, frogs. Should be a lovely day! Looking forward to catching some sun?" Vicious cheerily greeted his neighbors and received three hearty *croaks* in return.

"Must be your day off," the largest frog said. "Have a fine one!"

As Vicious skirted the pond, he sensed, more than saw, mice and salamanders flitting through the thick layer of leaves on the forest floor. Overhead, birds chipped and trilled, encouraging the emerging sunshine. Squirrels scolded as they leapt from branch to branch searching for their breakfast. Vicious heard rustling in the undergrowth. Perhaps a deer and her fawn were nearby. Usually when he was in the forest he was concentrating on the ground, looking for ingredients for Reynard. This morning, it was a treat to take time to appreciate the forest and creatures who lived in it.

BERT BUCK BUZZ

primeval residents, live at the pond at Three Frogs Hollow,
family relationships unknown

Now the sun was higher, and as the weasel proceeded on his journey, the landscape became more open. The mists and fog were gone. The sun brightened all it touched.

He passed through several small clearings, filled with clover and daisies. In one, he saw a family of cottontails feasting on blossoms and decided to pause and enjoy the sight. Not wanting to frighten the rabbits, Vicious sat at a respectful distance.

They seem so happy and carefree, Vicious thought, feeling a bit jealous. They casually nibbled blossoms and, from time to time, stopped to nuzzle each other. They had a brief nap, and Vicious nodded off too. Soon, though, he was awakened by the rabbits engaged in an exuberant game. They ran and jumped, chasing then backing off. One was taking a break with her back to the action when another suddenly jumped her from behind. They all honked with excitement! The noise concerned Vicious, as he was generally unfamiliar with rabbit vocalisations. Was one hurt? No—they were clearly having fun with each other. At the end of the game, they resumed feasting on the flowers, fully content with the sunshine, the delicious treats, and each other's company.

While Vicious was enjoying watching the rabbits, he unexpectedly felt sad. As he reflected on his feelings, he found himself idly picking flowers and braiding their stems together. The repetitive motion soothed him, and in a moment of clarity he realised how lonely he was. His family had broken up when he was so young, with his brothers and sisters striking out to make lives of their own. Vicious always felt he was made of different stuff. Perhaps he was not born to be a weasel. He certainly didn't feel ready to be living the weasel life on his own. But his mother, saying he was old enough, had gently—if such an action can be gentle—pushed him out of her burrow.

He had wandered for quite a while, eventually finding Reynard and, thankfully, a home and a job. His days were full, and he believed he was doing something important. Though his habit had been to push the feeling aside, he finally understood there was no denying his loneliness.

Vicious wondered why this insight should strike today. It threatened to mar his day off. *I imagine it's significant. But how?* With that, he turned his attentions back to his present surroundings and immersed himself in the joyful spirit of such a glorious day. He playfully formed his braid of wildflowers into a circlet and, with a smile, placed it on his head. Rising from his spot and bidding the rabbits a silent farewell, he continued on his way.

* * * * *

The boundary of the grounds at Milkweed Manor lay just ahead. Vicious easily jumped over the old low stone wall. Not far ahead, he spotted an animal whom he had seen a few times before but did not know personally. She had an intriguing masked face and a luxuriously thick, ringed tail. Strangely, she seemed to be excitedly scrounging through the manor's trash heap!

"Hello, there, miss!" Vicious called a greeting. The animal, not aware of anyone approaching, started in surprise. "Oh, I'm so sorry to frighten you. 'Vicious' here—yet perfectly harmless! Ha ha! 'Vicious' is my name, you see!"

For her part, Roxanne wasn't so sure about the 'harmless!' A weasel wearing a rumpled tunic, carrying a dirty pack sack, and crowned with a wreath of wildflowers? She'd never seen such a thing—not even close! Nonetheless, there he was, mere feet away, and this odd creature was smiling broadly, clearly expecting a reply.

"Hello, sir! No, I didn't hear you approaching. You are 'quite quiet,' to turn a phrase." Roxanne reasoned her safest approach would be to show no fear. "And wherever did you get that name? It's a little off-putting."

Vicious thought it was a somewhat personal question, but decided to answer anyway. "Well, since you ask, I'll tell you! I was the smallest of my litter." By long habit, he steadfastly avoided the distasteful term 'runt.' "My mother gave me this name as an encouragement to live up to my weasel nature. But despite the name, I've always had trouble being fierce. But enough about me! What are you doing?"

"The scullery maid at the Manor house discards all the manor's rubbish in this heap. And I must say that there are often quite nice things to be found. In our

"Hello there, Miss!" Vicious called a greeting.

community I run a little shop, the Mercantile, and as a sideline sometimes make clothes for the animals. Many of the items in my shop, as well as the fabrics I use in my sewing projects, come from this very heap! And truly, I find scrounging about quite absorbing, like a treasure hunt! I get out here as often as time and weather permit."

Intrigued, Vicious asked if he could join her.

"Suit yourself! It's not like I own this heap, so of course!" Roxanne went back to her work and soon they were both fully absorbed in the hunt. As her initial fears of this odd creature subsided, Roxanne began humming a little tune. It was simple enough, and after a bit Vicious picked it up and joined in. What a harmonious scene! An odd pair perhaps, but a seemingly compatible one. The two very different creatures clearly felt comfortable in each other's company, despite the raccoon's initial misgivings.

It wasn't long before Vicious found a few round objects. Roxanne identified them as 'buttons.' Having no use for them, he offered them to her, and she dropped them into her nearly full sack. Before Vicious arrived, she had already found several nice items, including a few ripped blouses of excellent quality silk, a stained camisole, and the most precious little beaded bag. The only damage was a broken chain which could be easily repaired. What a fabulous addition it would make to the inventory of the luxury section of her shop.

Her sack was soon full, yet she spotted still more items that it would be just too much of a shame to leave behind. "Oh, dear! There are so many lovely things here, but I don't have any more room in my sack!"

"I have a pack with me and it's nearly empty—just a few morels for my dinner! I'd be happy to carry some of your treasures for you if you don't mind my accompanying you back to your shop," Vicious said.

Normally Roxanne was cautious with strangers, but she couldn't bear to leave the lovely things she was finding behind. So, she accepted Vicious' generous offer—with a reservation. "Yes, thank you. But being a stranger, you must then be directly on your way!"

After combing through the heap a bit longer, Vicious could no longer contain his curiosity. "Roxanne, I hope you won't think me rude, but I'm wondering what kind of animal you are. I've never seen another like you! Your appearance is quite striking, by the way."

Roxanne smiled with her mouth, but the smile didn't reach her eyes.

"I must tell you, Vicious, for quite some time it was a mystery even to me. Why don't we take a seat and rest for a bit. I'll tell you what I know." With that, they settled on the low rock wall near the heap and she began the strange tale of her origins.

"My earliest memory is disturbing. I remember being trapped in a box made of metal bars. I was very young, afraid, and all alone, and have no idea how I came to be there. It was dark, and so cold. I was shivering uncontrollably. It was noisy in a rumbling scary way, noisy in a way I've never heard before or since."

"That's horrible, Roxanne!" Vicious longed to lay a comforting paw on her shoulder but held back for fear of offending a creature he barely knew.

Roxanne slumped a little. "I was in that box for a long time. Then there was an even louder noise and a huge bump. Someone put the box, with me in it, on a machine that moved me, still in the box, into a bright place where there was a crowd of humans.

"Two of them took me to what they called their house. They told me this was to be my home too and let me out of the box. I stayed in the house with them. They fed me well. They seemed to like me and spent a good bit of time talking to me and stroking my fur."

She paused, seeming to relive memories both pleasant and painful.

"Sometimes they had human guests. Usually the guests were quite taken with me, though I do remember one rather unfortunate scene. Anyway, it was a pleasant enough life, and I had fun wandering around the house. I especially liked opening things to see what was inside. I'm very good with my hands, you see." With that, she paused again, holding her paws out in front of her, turning them over, and regarding them closely. A thought had captured her attention, but she kept it to herself and returned to her story.

"So, to finally answer your question, the humans called me a 'raccoon.' I took that to mean raccoon is the kind of animal I am and not my personal name because that is 'Roxanne.' Judging from things they and their friends said over time, I came to understand that I was born a long way away and that raccoons didn't normally live in their part of the world. It was unlikely that I would ever meet another raccoon, and that made me sad. It still does when I think about it.

"And you know, Vicious, despite having the label 'raccoon,' I still don't know who I am or who I'm meant to be." Again, she paused, seemingly for introspection.

Vicious marveled at the strange—and sad—life Roxanne had led in her younger days, but still said nothing. He waited for her to pick up the tale in her own time.

"Once, when the humans were gone for the day, I thought I'd try to open the door in the kitchen and—much to my surprise—it opened! I was irresistibly drawn to go through the door and found myself in a garden. It was so pretty, with nicely clipped grass and colorful flowers and fresh air and, overhead, a china blue sky. I was enthralled. But when I wanted to go back in, I couldn't open the door! I tried everything, but it just wouldn't budge.

"Oh, Vicious, pardon me! You asked what kind of animal I am, and I already answered that. Now I'm just babbling!"

"No, it's fine! Please go on." Vicious was spellbound.

"I've never talked about this before, and it may do me some good." She hesitated before she continued. "So, there I was, locked out of the house. I decided to explore a little further and try the door again later, but before I knew it, I was lost. I tried to find my way back to the human's house, but just got hopelessly turned around. What could I do?

"I started wandering. It must have been three or four days—sometimes harrowing days, I might add—until I collapsed from exhaustion. Luckily, animals found me, kind caring animals, and brought me here. They invited me to be part of their community."

"There's a good ending, Roxanne, but overall I'd have to say it's a sad story, especially the part about being unlikely to ever meet another raccoon. You must be lonely." After a moment's thought, an emboldened Vicious added, "If you're lonely, then indeed that's something we have in common."

"How so?" Roxanne asked, her interest piqued.

"I'm a shaman's assistant and live at his isolated encampment deep in the forest. We're quite cut off from other animals, and, to make it even worse, I rarely get a day off. Don't get me wrong though, I'm grateful to have a home with Reynard, who is a most remarkable and admirable fox." Searching for a more cheerful note, he added, "This is one of my treasured days off, and what a nice day it is!"

Weasel and raccoon looked into each other's eyes for a moment. *Could I be so fortunate*, each thought, *as to have found a friend?*

* * * * *

After sitting in quiet contemplation for a few minutes, they got up and turned their attention back to the heap. Vicious soon found something wonderful. It was a metal disc with a loop at the top and a lovely design of entwined leaves on one side. As he turned it in his paw, it caught the sunshine, speckling his face with shards of reflected light. "What is it?" he asked as he handed it to Roxanne.

"It's so beautiful! I think it's a pendant. Female humans wear them for decoration. It should have a ribbon through this loop so that it can be tied around one's neck. It's quite a find!"

"You should have it, Roxanne, as you are clearly taken with it."

"No. I thank you, but it just wouldn't be right. You found it. You should keep it! It's very special."

He tucked the pretty 'pendant' in the pocket of his tunic, eager to show it to Reynard.

Late in the afternoon, both their sacks bulging with precious finds, the pair headed to Roxanne's Mercantile. It was but a quarter hour's walk from the low stone wall at the back of the Manor property, and as they went, they passed the time in pleasant conversation. From time to time, one of them said something clever and laughter rang through the forest. Too soon, their destination came into view.

At the Mercantile, Vicious unloaded Roxanne's finds from his pack. Honoring her wishes that he not linger, he thanked her for the lovely and enlightening afternoon and bid her farewell. As he turned to leave, he hesitated on her porch. "I'm glad I met you, Roxanne. I'm sorry for your traumatic younger life, but glad you've found a home here. Perhaps I'll see you again." He was pleased to see her smiling sweetly.

She could feel her cheeks flush. She had never told anyone her story before, but somehow this unlikely creature had prompted her to open her heart. And it was comforting to meet another creature who, like her, seemed to struggle with loneliness. "Goodbye, Vicious. Be safe, and if you ever find yourself nearby, be sure to stop in."

Vicious whistled all the way home, fingering the pendant in his pocket.

* * * * *

Over the next several weeks, each thought often of the other. Vicious replayed Roxanne's story of her early life. It was a remarkable tale, though there were many parts he didn't understand. He shared the highlights with Reynard, but the fox was unable to shed any light on either the lives of raccoons or the circumstances of the journey that had taken Roxanne to live with the two humans. As for Roxanne, she smiled each of the many times she recalled their walk from the heap back to the Mercantile—a walk enlivened by Vicious' clever conversation and rather silly jokes.

When the time finally came for his next eagerly anticipated day off, Vicious headed directly to the Mercantile.

Roxanne's ears perked up at a cheerful whistling sound and a few moments later saw him approaching. She smoothed her work apron and opened her door just as he was about to knock. "Vicious, how wonderful to see you! Come in, come in! We've much to catch up on."

Roxanne prepared tea and arranged a selection of biscuits on a hand-painted bone china plate. As they sat at the table enjoying their refreshment, Vicious recounted an adventure that he and Reynard had recently.

"My master and I were roaming the forest in search of cast-off snail shells. Reynard's typically at home in the forest. 'Know it like the back of my hand,' he has often boasted to me. But on this particular day he didn't seem to know it that well after all. We were walking through a dreary drizzle, single file with Reynard in the lead. We had gone a long way, and I was bored and not paying much attention. Suddenly Reynard screeched to a halt and screamed, 'BEAR!'"

Roxanne gasped at the image.

"Instantly whirling around, he crashed smack into me, knocking me down and running right over me in his haste to escape the giant fierce creature! I lay prone, my face smashed into the dirt, expecting to meet my maker at any moment. When nothing happened, I slowly opened my eyes and cautiously lifted my head. And what did I see—aside from no fox? A large, dark, vaguely bear-shaped...bush!"

"A bush!" Roxanne laughed so hard she nearly spilt her tea! And Vicious laughed too.

After conversing a while longer, she excused herself and fetched a bundle from the back room. She had wrapped it in tissue paper and her favorite red and white candy cane string. "This is for you!" Feeling suddenly a bit unsure of herself, she spoke softly. "I made it for you."

Vicious carefully untied the string and unwrapped the paper, revealing a poet's shirt! The material was a patchwork of many white and off-white fabrics. It was expertly sewn, and when he tried it on, it fit perfectly. He could barely speak.

"This is beautiful, Roxanne! I've never had anything nearly as nice." He stood tall and proud in his new clothes, still and silent for many moments, taking it all in. "I'm humbled you thought of me and used your time and considerable talents to make me something so special!"

"You look so handsome!" Roxanne beamed.

Blushing, he replied "Well, Roxanne, I have something for you too!" Vicious reached into the pocket of the tunic he had worn and closed his paw around the surprise. Then, stretching his arm out towards Roxanne, opened it to reveal the pendant he had found at the trash heap! But it was different. There was a large translucent blue stone in the center and smaller clear crystals set around the edge.

"Reynard helped me make it. This is no longer a simple pendant but is now a magical talisman. It will help keep you safe. If there is danger nearby, the blue stone in the middle will glow, and one of the crystals around the edge will flash showing the direction in which danger lies."

Vicious pressed the pendant into Roxanne's paw.

"To be honest, I've worried about you spending so much time on the manor grounds. The humans there, especially Cook and her nasty husband, the groundskeeper, are not friendly to the animals of the forest!"

Roxanne gazed at the pendant, transfixed. Her eyes sparkling, she reached into a nearby basket and drew out a ribbon. It was robin's egg blue, nearly matching the center stone. She threaded the ribbon through the loop at the top of the talisman and asked Vicious to tie it round her neck, a task which he happily, but barely, managed. He was embarrassed, and his paws trembled badly.

The talisman was stunning on Roxanne, and she was so pleased with her gift she positively glowed!

They passed the afternoon enjoying each other's company. When the time came for Vicious to leave, they gave each other a friendly hug and parted, looking forward to seeing each other again.

* * * * *

A few days later, Roxanne was back at the Manor's trash heap gathering treasures, concentrating on her search and oblivious to what was around her. Suddenly, the blue stone in the middle of her talisman glowed brightly, and the crystal on the left flashed an urgent warning. Her eyes widened and she glanced around. Out of the

This is beautiful, Roxanne! I've never had anything nearly as nice!"

corner of her eye, nearly too late, she caught the shadow of the groundskeeper. He was raising a rifle from his side!

Faster than she knew she could move, Roxanne sprinted to the low wall at the edge of the grounds. Just as a loud gunshot cracked through the afternoon stillness, she sailed over the wall and in a single, smooth motion landed in a roll on the ground on the other side, stunned and bruised, but unharmed.

As she lay on the ground, she clutched the talisman in her quivering paws. She lay there until she recovered her composure, then sat up. Having found nothing truly special today at the trash heap, and feeling a little bit light-headed, she decided to leave her pack where she dropped it and retrieve it another day. As she slowly made her way back to her flat above the Mercantile, she reflected, despite the day's traumatic event, on her good fortune. *Having a friend saved my life. And I think having a friend will change my life, in small ways as well as big ones. I'm looking forward to that!*

*A turning point can be so obvious it smacks
you in the face. Or it can be so subtle, so
fleeting, so soft-spoken that it awaits discovery
in hindsight.*

In Which Nothing Much Happens

The day was quiet at the Inn at Ivy Knoll. It had been many a year since the road passing Milkweed Manor had been moved a few miles south, and that move made all the difference. Nowadays, at Ivy Knoll, a quiet day was not the exception, but the norm.

The building was rumored to have been a human children's playhouse generations ago. Though no one knew exactly when hares had taken possession, it was clear they had been living there for generations. Glenna's parents had inherited the inn from her maternal grandfather, and Glenna had been born here.

Over the years, as time and means permitted, the various hare owners added to the original stone structure. The result of this disjointed construction activity was a sprawling building that had clearly had no blueprint. But it was full of charm. Repairing the damage from past storms had created a patchwork of various colors and shapes of roof tiles. And the roof itself sported a jumble of chimneys, some round and some square, each puffing smoke from a cozy fireplace that warmed a cheerful room. The windows weren't all the same, some being single panes of glass and others mullioned in a more old-fashioned style. The shutters were a unique feature in that they were all the same. Evie had recently replaced them to better protect the inn from storms. She'd painted them a merry true red, striking any time of year but perfect for the holidays.

Graham and Glenna had, in their prime, worked hard at the inn. But now infirmity severely limited their activities, and it fell to Evie to keep the place afloat and her parents cared for. She was their youngest, and the only child still living at home. One by one, her brothers and sisters had left to build their lives elsewhere. Though her next eldest sibling was hesitant to leave Evie with the burden of running the inn and caring for their parents, he left anyway.

Sometimes Evie wished she, too, could have the adventure of an exciting new life. She heard many tales from the few guests who occasionally visited the inn and hung on every word. Sometimes, as she lay in bed at night, she would rehearse those tales in her mind and wonder, *what would it be like to venture out into the wide world?* But she knew she was needed here, so here she stayed.

Evie had a lot on her shoulders, but, truly, she loved every minute at the old inn. There was a lot of work to do, and she couldn't always keep up, especially with building maintenance. As a result, the structure was getting a bit shabby here and there. But to Evie, a bit of peeling paint or a slightly sagging windowsill only added to the place's charm.

As the building aged, the need for repairs seemed to accelerate, and sometimes Evie worried. At the same time, she understood age was the inn's friend. It was only with age that the ivy had grown to nearly cover the walls. It was time that cloaked the rock wall with moss in the most vivid shades of green. Likewise, it was time that grew the wisteria over the front porch into a spectacular spring display of lavender. And it was time that encouraged the yellow roses to sprawl over the arch at the gate. True, last season's big storm had inflicted severe damage to those roses, but they were already recovering, and time would restore them to their former glory.

The inn was such a lovely spot that many of the animals chose to have family or community celebrations here. And Evie, who had loved to bake from the day she learned the art as a young girl, had recently converted the parlor into a charming café serving tea and delectable homemade scones, muffins, and special daily treats. Spiced carrot scones were her most popular bake and so well loved that some of the community's residents could barely last a day without one!

Between special events and the café, Evie and her parents lived securely and at the same time, provided the community's residents a welcoming place to just hang out.

Felicia, now a regular visitor to the community, knew there was an event at the inn today and arrived early. As she often did, she brought a tub of butter pilfered from the Manor kitchen as her, or, more accurately, the Manor's unwitting contribution. Having devoured not one, not two, but three buttered scones and tea with cream (hold the tea!) she was busy cat napping in her favorite spot on the mossy wall.

* * * * *

Back at Rosebud Cottage, it was a busy morning. A recent streak of bad weather had kept the squirrels inside. While they kept busy reading, drawing, baking, and enjoying other indoor activities, the weeds in the garden were up to no good. At least no good for the squirrel family. The uninvited plants were thriving, growing larger and stronger day by rainy day to the point they were threatening to choke out Emma's precious herbs. This morning, the run of bad weather had broken, and it promised to be a fine day, mainly sunny but with large cotton clouds sailing across the deep blue sky.

The girls knew their mama had an engagement today and proposed to pull the weeds while she was gone. It was early, but they were already working in the garden. Emma was in the kitchen packing two totes with everything she would need for the day. The Wee Scouts would meet at the inn, and Emma was going to teach them their second lesson about native plants.

A bluebird streaked by the window. The flash of color caught her attention, and as she looked up, saw the girls concentrating on their tasks. *How sweet they are in their garden smocks and hats.* She wrapped her shoulders with her lightest shawl, grabbed the totes, one over her right shoulder and the other in her right paw, and headed out the door and down the path.

"'Bye, girls! See you late this afternoon."

"'Bye, Mama! Love you!"

"Love you more!"

* * * * *

It was a pleasant walk from Rosebud Cottage to the Inn. Emma found Evie in the kitchen baking the morning's second batch of scones, Felicia having devoured a good portion of the first.

"Oh, Evie! Those scones smell scrumptious—as always! The spices are sensational! What's your secret ingredient? Smells a bit like nutmeg."

Evie just rolled her eyes, laughed, and gave Emma a big hug. It was a running joke between the two for Emma to ask for the secret and Evie to reply, 'Well, it wouldn't be a secret if I told you, would it?' They'd replayed that banter so many times.

"It's a blessing the weather's turned for the better. Should be a good turnout," Evie said. "Are you ready?"

"Oh, yes, and looking forward to it. The little ones are always so much fun. I love how wide their eyes get when something surprises them."

"And the squeals and squeaks when they're startled! Their youthful energy is so good for Mum and Dad, you know." Evie glanced out the window to check on

"Oh, Evie! Those scones smell scrumptious-as usual!"

Glenna and Graham who were relaxing in their rockers on the porch. "Oh, and afterwards, Dad's going to teach them how to tie a fancy knot!"

"The little ones will love that!" Emma smiled. "Sophie and Carmen certainly are doing a great service for Littleton Hedge."

Prior to Felicia's relocation program, which had populated Littleton Hedge with many mice, Sophie and Carmen lived with their parents and their younger siblings as the single mouse family in the community. Now the hedge teemed with tiny residents. The sisters adored the younger mice and had determined to establish a chapter of the Wee Scouts for the little ones. The Wee Scouts, or "Wee Ones" as they were sometimes called, was a highly respected national organization diligently working for the welfare and education of young animals.

The troop Sophie and Carmen had organized, Troop Milkweed, was a godsend. Keeping the children busy and happy improved family harmony and helped shape the good citizens and leaders of the future. The young mice worked on projects and earned badges which they sewed on the colorful sashes Roxanne helped them make. Of the scouts' many activities, they especially enjoyed the field trips. For Itsy, who was Sophie and Carmen's next-door neighbor, there was a special bonus. Though Itsy was younger than they, sometimes the older girls invited her to help plan events and programs for the troop. Itsy felt so important!

* * * * *

The kitchen timer dinged. As Evie pulled the fresh batch of scones out of the oven, she looked up to see the Wee Scouts arriving for their much-anticipated field trip. Each wore a crisp blue uniform and a brightly coloured badge sash. The troop was fairly new, so not many badges had yet been earned, but the scouts were proud of their fine sashes nonetheless!

Sophie, carrying a basket, was in the lead with Carmen bringing up the rear. Their charges were bouncing about, excited about the outing and looking forward to earning points towards both their 'Out and About' and 'Forest Safety' badges.

On their way, the mice had discovered a berry patch fully loaded with fruit and thought a basket of juicy ripe berries would be a nice present for their hostess. The leaders' paws were full restraining the little ones from eating too much of the fruit themselves. But somehow, the mice managed to both fill the basket and avoid tummy aches!

As the scouts settled in the shade of the inn's garden, Sophie took the basket to Evie. She was delighted with the gift. "The berries will be a lovely accompaniment to the scones! Please thank the little ones for me!"

Sophie selected one of the carrot scones to divide among her charges, who were now sitting in a circle noisily chatting about their walk and pointing out particularly beautiful features of the inn's garden—the snapdragons were spectacular this time of year.

Adding to the cheery mood of the day, birds sang in the trees, and dragonflies swirled over the little pond in the corner of the garden. Goldfish broke the surface in glistening rings, and one of the mice was happily sharing crumbs from her piece of scone with them. The sunshine was warm on their upturned faces as others made a game of identifying shapes in the slowly drifting clouds. "I see a bird!" "I see a giant dragon!" "Eek eek!" the rest squealed in mock terror.

All the while, Thea had been sitting nearby at an outdoor café table. She was absorbed in one of her favorite books. Being an owl, she had excellent peripheral vision and spotted the basket of berries the instant it appeared. Jumping to her feet, she rushed to the café window. The owl made a show of refreshing her tea and placing another scone on her plate before getting to her actual goal—a generous helping of deep red berries. Returning to her table, she nibbled on her treats and continued her reading. Soon she was lost in a particularly engaging volume, *Owl Wisdom of the Ancients*.

Undisturbed by the excited voices, Glenna and Graham, quite comfortable in their rocking chairs on the inn's expansive porch, had fallen asleep. Evie and Emma sat near them waiting for the event to begin whilst enjoying a cup of tea—with cream and lemon, please, and don't hold the tea! Emma didn't understand the joke but smiled anyway.

* * * * *

A distant whistling caught Evie's attention. It drew closer and closer, and she recognized Colwyn's voice well before he appeared at the rose arch.

"Greetings, everyone! What a fine day!" All the mice squealed in delight and scampered to wrap their tiny arms around their hero's legs, led, of course, by Itsy. Colwyn, a rat, was a super-hero-sized mouse in the young one's eyes. They utterly idolized him.

"Greetings to you too, Colwyn." Evie smiled as Colwyn gently detached himself from the scouts and approached the group on the porch. "You're looking sharp today!" Evie put her hands on her hips and gave the rat an approving look. "Your usual?"

"Yes, please. I've been looking forward to a scone of yours ever since I heard about this event! Is it time for Emma's presentation?"

"Not quite yet. Let's give the mice a while longer to finish their snack, then, on with the show!"

* * * * *

Having time to kill and spotting Felicia lying on the nearby stone wall, Colwyn decided to chat with his friend until the presentation began. The cat sensed him approaching and roused herself with a wide yawn. Then, standing on the wall, she arched her back, stretched her arms in front of her, and her legs beneath her in a perfect downward dog pose. *Umm. Feels good.*

"How've you been, Felicia?" Colwyn inquired. "It's been a while since I've seen you!"

"Indeed! And I've missed you and the rest of my friends here in the community. I was a bit under the weather for a while there, but all better now. I thought Emma's presentation would be a great opportunity to see all of you again. Sure hope I don't end up napping through it though! This wall, with the soft moss and dappled shade, is just not the place to perch if you want to stay awake!"

"Ha! I know that well enough, my friend!" Colwyn answered. "I've enjoyed many a lazy afternoon in this very spot! And what could be better after one of Evie's excellent scones?"

"Nothing I know of! I've had three! And with butter! But tell me, what's the news from the community?" Felicia asked.

"Oh, probably nothing that you don't already know. The recently arrived mice have us on our toes! Once we realised they needed new skills for life here in the forest, we put together a training program. It's going quite well. The young ones are often more open to new ideas than the adults, so Sophie and Carmen are including the lessons in their Wee Scouts program."

"Yes," Felicia confessed, "I must say I feel remiss in not realizing the possible problems of a new and different environment when I began relocating them. I was convinced I was doing the right thing moving them out of range of the reprehensible Cook and her vitriolic scullery maid. But then the young ones got so sick! Thank

Colwyn decided to chat with his friend.

goodness Reynard and Vicious were able to help. It could have been a real tragedy. I never would have forgiven myself!"

Colwyn paused, turning his attention to the cat herself. "Well, it's working out fine, and you, Felicia, have much to be proud of. You've saved many lives! But you know, I've often worried about you living in such a negative environment. It can't be good for your spirits, dear friend. Why do you stay? You must know you'd be more than welcome in the community."

"I know." She paused. "As for why, I suppose there's more than one reason. Despite her many huge and glaring faults, I do still feel gratitude to Cook for saving my life. I've no doubt I would've been dead within the day if she hadn't, despite her selfish motives, taken me from the street. Then there are the mice. Fewer and fewer venture into the manor house these days, but still, there's that occasional stray who needs my help."

"You've more than repaid your debt to Cook. And you've already saved so many lives. You can't save them all, you know! At some point you need to put yourself first."

"Well, yes, Colwyn, I agree in principle. But there's one more reason. You are aware of Cook, the scullery maid, and the groundskeeper. But there's another human living at the manor, old Lord Grimsley. I don't see him often because Cook doesn't want me wandering beyond the kitchen. But, as you know, I don't always pay attention to Cook's rules!

"He's very good to me. He talks to me and pets me. Sometimes, when he's sitting in his rocking chair in the conservatory, with his wool throw—it's so soft—over his legs, he invites me to lie in his lap and he strokes me and talks to me. He tells me I'm a good kitty. Or a pretty kitty."

"I never knew of him!"

"That doesn't surprise me, Colwyn, as I lived at the manor for many months before I knew he was there. Anyway, those times lying in Grimsley's lap—that's what I call him, though I know it's taking liberties—are the best I've ever had. Well, I take that back, because I do have vague memories of being with my mum and siblings when I was very young, and those times were wonderful, before we got so hungry and sick, that is. But back to the present. A little bit of his kind treatment goes a long way towards neutralizing the effects of Cook's nastiness."

"You're a sweet and kind soul, Felicia, and I'm so glad you have that comfort. You deserve it!"

"To tell you the truth, I'm worried I won't have it much longer. I see Grimsley less and less frequently, and when I do see him, he seems weaker. Sometimes I'm with him when Cook brings his supper. I hide under his chair so she doesn't see me, because if she did, her shrieks might well give the old gentleman a heart attack! Anyway, I've noticed he eats very little."

Colwyn considered for a moment. "That's certainly worrying. But you yourself told me you were under the weather a while ago. Yet look at you now! Fit as a fiddle! Lord Grimsley may well recover too. And I don't think it's overly optimistic to say 'probably' will."

Felicia dearly hoped that was the case.

"Oh, excuse me, Felicia. Here's Emma. Must be time to start the program." As he walked away, Felicia settled down to watch the presentation, or to resume her nap as the case may be!

* * * * *

Colwyn and Emma approached the group of seated Wee Ones. Colwyn addressed the gathering.

"It's good to see everyone in fine spirits on this lovely day. Ready to learn more about forest safety? You all know Emma, so let's get started!"

The mice clapped, and a few of the more boisterous ones whistled as Emma, carrying her two totes, stepped to the front.

"I trust you all remember what you learned last time about edible plants of the forests and meadows. Next time we'll wrap up with mystical qualities of plants. But for today, we're concentrating on medicinal plants."

Emma was skilled at weaving interesting tales into her educational talks and had the mice's full attention—not an easy accomplishment. One by one, she introduced six extraordinary plants. She passed around samples and told how the plant could help with an injury or illness. Sophie gave each of the mice a pencil and a map of the surrounding area. As Emma discussed where each plant could be found—that is, whether it lived in the forest or in a meadow, in sun or in shade, and so on—the mice made notes on their maps.

Plants that helped heal injuries were clearly the group's favorite. Each mouse selected a buddy and practiced using the plant on an imagined injury. It was great fun fooling with the strips of bandaging, and, of course, there's always a joker ready to tie up his buddy!

At the end of the program, Emma gave a quiz. When everyone was finished, she read the answers aloud so each mouse could check his buddy's paper. Everyone passed, some more spectacularly than others! It was another step towards the 'Forest Safety' badge!

* * * * *

Carmen thanked Emma for another entertaining and enlightening talk, then turned to the mice. "Come with me! Granddad Graham has a surprise for you!" She led them to the porch where the elderly hares were waiting in their rocking chairs. From a basket in her lap, Glenna pulled a short length of rope for each mouse and instructed the little ones to find places to sit so they could all see Graham clearly.

Graham didn't wait for them to settle down—he knew that could be a long wait. Instead, he sat tall in his chair and dramatically displayed his piece of rope in front of him, one end in each paw. With quick movements of his arms, the length of rope, as if by magic, transformed into a beautiful, intricate knot. Admiring gasps from those who had been paying attention quickly directed all mouse eyes to the elderly hare, who repeated the trick once more.

"How ever did you do that?" squeaked Itsy.

"Watch carefully. I'll do it more slowly." He tied, untied, and retied the knot a few more times, then said, "Now do it with me! Everyone, hold your rope in front of you, like this!" Glenna scanned the group, signaling Emma to help anyone who was having a problem.

Graham continued in this manner step-by-step, and soon each Wee One had an amazingly beautiful knot. They tied the knots again and again, and before long most had mastered the Celtic square knot.

"Do we get badge points?" one of the youngsters asked.

Sophie said she'd check the Wee Scout Leader's Manual to see if there were a relevant badge.

"But for now," Carmen continued, "it's time to be on our way. Everyone, let's take a minute to clean up after ourselves. Anybody know why?"

One of the youngsters squeaked, "To be good guests and good citizens!" He had been working on his 'Good Citizen' badge.

* * * * *

"Watch carefully. I'll do it more slowly.

The clean-up was quick and efficient. "Good job! Now let's all give our gracious hosts, Evie, Graham, and Glenna, a big 'thank you' for such a wonderful day."

The scouts squeaked a loud, excited thank you. A few blew kisses, which the hares made a show of catching and blowing back! The mice gathered their belongings, lined up between Sophie at the head and Carmen at the rear, and set out on their return journey to Littleton Hedge.

Colwyn watched the mice pass through the rose-covered arch. "Sophie and Carmen are doing a fine job with this scout program. It's just what the community needed—a way to educate the mice children about safety in their new environment—but with a big dose of fun."

"Yes," added Emma. "And the incentive of earning the badges is brilliant!"

"And," Evie said "the children's knowledge rubs off on the adults. Everyone benefits."

The energy level at the Inn subsided substantially with the troop's departure. Glenna and Graham responded by resuming their naps. Emma and Evie joined them on the porch, relaxing over a cup of chamomile tea.

Colwyn thought of continuing his conversation with Felicia, but saw she was sound asleep. *I wonder how much of the presentation she saw*, he chuckled to himself. Then he spotted Thea seated at one of the café tables, her beak deep in a book. "Mind if I join you?"

"Of course not, Colwyn. Come sit! Your company's most welcome!" She closed her book, marking her place with a bookmark of pressed violets, her favorite flower since the day after the storm when the squirrel girls had found her. "I've read enough for today."

Colwyn chose a chair at Thea's table, gazing admiringly at her book. It seemed to command his attention. Somehow, he knew it was important. "What do you mean, 'read?'"

"Do you not know about reading and writing? It's one of life's true pleasures!" She opened her book and showed Colwyn the marks on the pages. She explained that the marks had special meaning for those who knew how to understand them. "The understanding is called 'reading.' But of course, before anyone can 'read' the marks, someone has to make them! Making the marks is called 'writing!'

"The marks can be put together in different ways so the writer can record any type of information and a reader—or many readers—can read it later. This book, for example, tells about the lives of famous owls who lived a long time ago."

"Do you have other books?"

"I don't have many yet. But I'm adding to my collection whenever I can. So far, all of them are about owls, like the special places they live, or the adventures they have, or even owl love stories!"

Colwyn immediately understood the marks were magic. He closed his eyes and, for quite some time, considered this new idea. Thea thought he had fallen asleep and was reaching for her book when his eyelids flickered. A smile spread across Colwyn's face, and he slowly opened his eyes.

"'Reading' and 'writing.' Yes, I want to learn that. Will you teach me, Thea?"

"I'd be honored."

It seemed that nothing much had happened at the Inn at Ivy Knoll that day. But not so for Colwyn. He'd found what he was born to do. He would learn to read and write. He would chronicle the stories of his beloved adoptive home—the community in the forest behind Milkweed Manor. He would share them with the world, and the world would never be the same.

finis

To My Readers

Dear Reader,

Thank you so much for allowing me to share these stories with you. They were a joy to write and illustrate. To tell the truth, as I read back over these tales it surprises me that I could write them. Where did they come from? Well, the whole experience was a giant exercise in imagination, and I think that's why I liked it so much and was able to stick with it. Someone asked me where I am when I write. My first answer was "In the big soft chair in the living room. But then I realized I was actually in the forest behind Milkweed Manor with the animals.

Whatever projects you may have, I urge you to complete them and enjoy the process. What you create will be your unique voice, and the world needs it!

I'd love to hear from you, not just your reactions to Milkweed Manor, but also what you're working on and what's special to you. My mailing address is on the copyright page at the beginning of the book. You can also reach me through:

e-mail at kspoole@hughes.net

my Etsy shop at www.etsy.com/shop/thefoxesgarden

my website, www.KaarenPoole.com

or on Facebook, www.facebook.com/MilkweedManor or

www.facebook.com/KaarenPooleArt

or on Instagram, www.instagram.com/KaarenPoole

I publish a monthly e-mail newsletter that I think you'd enjoy. You can sign up either by visiting my website or e-mailing you. Look forward to hearing from you!

Acknowledgements

I had so much help creating this book. Special thanks, first and foremost, to my sister Michele who endured many months of chatter about the characters and stories, helped me untangle knots in the plot, encouraged me when I lost my mojo, and, most of all, graciously did a detailed beta read for me – an invaluable contribution.

Throughout 2018, Nikol Rogers' coaching for creatives gave me the confidence and resolve to tackle this project. Then this year, Audrey Hughey, and the members of her Facebook group, The Author Transformation Alliance, provided encouragement, support, and information on every facet of the self-publishing process. This book could never have come to print without Audrey's help. Fortunately, I did most of the writing blissfully oblivious of all the steps and technologies of not only producing but marketing a book. When I joined Audrey's group and became aware of my ignorance and overwhelmed at all I'd have to learn, Audrey was there to help.

Thank you to my beta readers who generously gave their time and attention to reading and commenting on my draft. And thank you to my editor, Josiah Davis, who polished my manuscript and helped make it the best it could be.

Thanks to all my friends and family who encouraged and supported me. And thanks to all the animals I've ever had in my life. Their magical presence taught me so much and opened my eyes to how much love and beauty there is in this world.

Get Involved, Get Active

As an animal lover, there are many ways you can help our non-human brothers and sisters. One way is to support animal welfare organizations. Support, of course, can include donations or adoptions. But even being a follower on Facebook and bringing the work of these organization to the attention of your friends and acquaintances is so helpful. Here are a few of my favorites, all of which have nice Facebook pages.:

Idaho Black Bear Rehab

Hare Preservation Trust

Badger Trust

Best Friends

Your local wildlife rehab group—mine is Sierra Wildlife Rescue

There are so many more, and I urge you to pick your favorite animal then search for worthy organizations that work on their behalf.

And Finally, About the Author (on the right)

Since retiring from a career in Information Technology, I have put my energy into visual arts. I began with painting, but soon discovered many other media and loved them all! I opened my Etsy shop about five years ago and have enjoyed finding new homes for my work which is, regardless of the medium, nearly always animal themed.

For the past year I've focused on writing and illustrating this book and, in the process found I'm very happy as an author/illustrator. In fact, I have other books in mind, including sequels to this one, and I've already started on the second book in the series.

Aside from writing and creating visual art, I've become an avid gardener. With the exception of a few tomato plants and herbs, my garden is flower territory. I have about 35 rose bushes, and each year I grow dozens of annuals for cut flowers from seed. Seeing those seed sprouts and grow into full blooming plants is magic! And the bouquets I have in my house throughout the spring, summer, and most of the fall, are food for the soul.

I am so grateful to have animals in my life. This is me with my dog Fiona. We also live with cats, rats, guinea pigs, a chicken, and ducks. My sister lives next door and she has a dog, cats, and a horse. There are always animal chores to do, and travel is difficult, but I couldn't imagine being without these amazing, generous-hearted, and often comical beings.